Alice Cherbonnel, Ernest Redwood

My Uncle And My Curee

Alice Cherbonnel, Ernest Redwood

My Uncle And My Curee

ISBN/EAN: 9783743373211

Manufactured in Europe, USA, Canada, Australia, Japa

Cover: Foto ©Andreas Hilbeck / pixelio.de

Manufactured and distributed by brebook publishing software (www.brebook.com)

Alice Cherbonnel, Ernest Redwood

My Uncle And My Curee

MY UNCLE AND MY CURÉ

TRANSLATED FROM THE FRENCH

OF

JEAN DE LA BRÈTE

By ERNEST REDWOOD

ILLUSTRATED BY GEORGES JANET

NEW YORK
DODD, MEAD AND COMPANY
1892

𝔘niversity 𝔓ress:
JOHN WILSON AND SON, CAMBRIDGE.

MY UNCLE AND MY CURÉ.

CHAPTER I.

I AM so small that one might call me a dwarf, were
not my head, my feet, and my hands in perfect proportion to my figure. My face has neither the undue
length nor the absurd breadth which one associates with
dwarfs, and with deformed persons in general; and the
daintiness of my extremities would be envied by more
than one beautiful woman.

Nevertheless, my diminutive figure has made me pour
out tears in secret. I say in secret, because my liliputian

body encloses a soul haughty, proud, and incapable of showing its wounds to the first comer, — above all, to my aunt. Such at least was my way of thinking when I was fifteen. But the incidents, the troubles, the cares, the joys, — in a word, the affairs, — of life have broadened rapidly characters much more rigid than mine.

My aunt was the most disagreeable woman I have ever known. She was very ugly, so far as I could judge, who had seen nothing, and had no standard of comparison.

Beside her I had the appearance of a gnat, of an ant. When I spoke to her I had to raise my head as high as if I wished to examine the top of a poplar. She was of plebeian origin, and like many of that class considered physical strength above everything, and professed for my puny person a disdain which crushed me.

Her disposition was a faithful copy of her physique. It was made up of irregularities, asperities, and sharp corners, against which the unfortunates who lived with her ran every day.

My uncle, a country gentleman whose stupidity had become a proverb in the place, had married her through weakness of mind and character. He died a short time after his marriage, and I never knew him. When I came to think it over, I attributed his premature death to my aunt, who seemed to me strong enough to put speedily underground not only one poor fellow, like my uncle, but a whole regiment, even, of husbands.

I was two years old when my parents went to the other world, leaving me to the caprice of the events of life and of my relatives. They left a goodly remnant of a large fortune, about four hundred thousand francs in land, which brought in a very fair revenue.

My aunt consented to bring me up. She did not love children, but she was poor, — for her husband had managed his affairs badly, — and she bethought her with satisfaction that comfort would come into her house with me.

What an ugly house, — large, dilapidated, built in the midst of a court full of manure, mud, fowls, and rabbits! Behind stretched a garden in which all the plants in creation crowded one another, pell-mell, without any one caring for them the least in the world. I believe that in the memory of man no one had seen a gardener trim the trees or weed out the useless plants, which increased according to their fancy, while it never occurred to my aunt and me to busy ourselves with them.

This virgin forest displeased me, because even as a child I had an innate taste for order.

The place was called Buisson. It was situated in the heart of the country, half a league from the church and a little village of some twenty thatched cottages. Neither château, castle, nor manor was within five leagues in any direction. We lived in the most complete isolation. My aunt sometimes went to C——, the town nearest Buisson. I wished keenly to go with her, consequently she never took me.

The only incidents in our life were the arrival of the farmers, who brought their indebtedness or their rents, and the visits of the curé.

Oh, what an excellent man the curé was! He came to the house three times a week, having undertaken, in a moment of great zeal, to cram my head with all the learning known to him.

He followed up his task with perseverance, although I understood how to put his patience to the test. Not that I was a blockhead, — I learned easily; but laziness was my darling sin. I loved it, I coddled it, in spite of the curé's expenditure of eloquence and the many efforts he made to tear this plant of Satan from my soul.

Then, and this was the most serious point, my ability to argue developed rapidly. I entered into discussions which irritated the curé; I assumed opinions which often offended and clashed with his dearest convictions.

It was a keen pleasure to me to contradict him, to tease him, to take a stand opposed to his ideas, his tastes, his arguments. This stirred my blood and kept my mind on the alert. I suspect that he had the same feeling, and that he would have been in despair had I lost all at once my cavilling ways and my independence of thought.

But I never laid them aside, because when I saw him stir in his seat, run his hands through his hair in despair, and smear his nose with snuff, — forgetting all the laws of propriety, a forgetfulness that came only when the case was serious, — nothing could equal my satisfaction.

Nevertheless, if he alone had been concerned, I fancy that I should sometimes have resisted the demon of a tempter. My aunt had taken the baleful habit of being present at the lessons, although she understood nothing, and yawned ten times an hour.

Contradiction, even when her ugly self was not concerned, put her in a fury, — a fury all the greater that she did not dare to say anything before the curé. Then, to see me argue seemed to her something abnormal in the physical and moral order of things. I never attacked her directly, because she was brutal and I feared her blows. Lastly, my voice— though I flatter myself that it is sweet and musical — produced upon her auditory nerves a disastrous effect.

In such case it will be understood that it was impossible, absolutely impossible, for me not to be malicious enough to set to work to enrage my aunt and torment my curé.

Nevertheless I loved him, — this poor curé. I loved him dearly; and I know that in spite of my absurd arguments, which sometimes reached impertinence, he had the greatest affection for me. I was not only the chosen one of his flock, I was the child of his adoption, his work, the daughter of his heart and mind. With this paternal affection was blended a tinge of admiration for my capabilities, my words, and my acts in general.

He had taken his task to heart. He had sworn to instruct me, to watch over me as a guardian angel, notwithstanding my obstinacy, my logic, and my whims. And this task had at once become the sweetest thing in his life, the greatest, if not the only, distraction in his monotonous existence.

Through rain, wind, snow, hail, heat, cold, and storms, I used to see the curé appear, his cassock tucked up to his knees, and his hat under his arm. I do not know that in all my life I ever saw him with his hat on. He had a way of walking with head uncovered, smiling at the passers-by, at the birds, at the trees, at the blades of grass. Round and plump, he seemed to rebound from the ground which he trod with a quick step, and to which he seemed to say, "You are good, and I love you." He was happy to be living, content with himself and with all the world. His kindly face, ruddy and fresh, surrounded with white hair, used to recall those late roses which still blossom under the first snows.

When he entered the court, fowls and rabbits ran at his voice to nibble some crusts of bread which he had been careful to slip into his pocket before leaving the *presbytère*. Perrine, the milkmaid, made a courtesy; then Suzon, the cook, hastened to open the door and show him into the salon, where we took our lessons.

My aunt, planted in an armchair with the grace of

a rather thick lightning-rod, rose at his approach, bade him welcome with a surly air, and began at a gallop on the subject of my misdeeds. After which, seating herself as stiff as a poker, she took her knitting, her favourite cat on her knees, and awaited, or did not await, an occasion to say something disagreeable to me.

The worthy curé heard with patience her harsh, ear-piercing voice. He shrugged his shoulders as if the reprimand were for him, and threatened me with his finger, half laughing. *Dieu merci*, he had known my aunt a long time! We settled ourselves at a little table which we placed near the window. This position had a twofold advantage, in that it removed us far enough from my aunt, who sat in state near the hearth at the end of the room, and at the same time allowed my eyes to follow the flights of the swallows and the flies, and in winter to note the effect of the snow and the hoar-frost on the trees of the garden.

The curé placed his snuff-box beside him, a checked handkerchief on the arm of his chair, and the lesson began.

When my laziness had not been too great, every-thing went well, at least while he was correcting my exercises; for although they were as short as possible, they were always done with care. My handwriting was clear and my style easy. The curé would nod his head with an air of satisfaction, take snuff enthusiastically, and say over and over, "Good! very good!"

During this time I was mentally counting the spots on his cassock, and asking myself how he would appear if he had a black wig, tight breeches, and a coat of red velvet like that which my great-uncle wore in his portrait.

The idea of the curé in breeches and a wig was so amusing that I would break out in a loud laugh. Then my aunt would cry,—

"Idiot! little stupid!"

And utter other amenities of this sort which were privileged as parliamentary, as well as explicit.

The curé would look at me, smiling, and say two or three times over,—

"Ah, youth, happy youth!"

And a reminiscence of himself at fifteen would make him half emit a sigh.

After this we passed to the recitation, and matters did not go so well. This was the critical time, the time for talk, for personal opinions, for discussions, not to say almost disputes.

The curé admired the men of antiquity, the heroes, and the almost fabulous deeds in which physical courage had played an important part. This preference was strange, because the curé was not exactly of the stuff of which heroes are made.

I had noticed that he did not at all like to go home at night; and this discovery, while it made me more fond of him, because I was a great coward

myself, left me no illusion on the subject of his courage.

For this good, peaceful, tranquil soul, lover of repose, of routine, of his flock and of his own self, had never, no, never, dreamed of being a martyr. I have seen him pale, at least as much as his red cheeks could pale, on reading the accounts of the tortures inflicted on the early Christians. He considered it a fine thing to enter heaven with the stride of a hero, but he thought it much pleasanter to advance peacefully toward eternity, without fatigue and without haste. He had not those exaltations which inspire a desire for death in order to see the sooner the Lord of worlds and time. No, not at all! He had made up his mind to go without a murmur when his time came; but he was sincerely desirous that this should be as distant as possible.

I confess that my temperament, which does not shine in the heroic line, disposes itself after the same sweet and comfortable fashion.

Nevertheless, he clung to his heroes; he admired them, extolled them, and loved them doubtless the more that, the opportunity being offered, he knew it absolutely impossible for him to imitate them.

As for me, I shared neither his tastes nor his enthusiasms. I experienced a profound antipathy to the Greeks and Romans. Through some subtile working of my fantastic intelligence, I had made up

my mind that these latter resembled my aunt, — or
that my aunt resembled them, as you please; and
from the day when I decided that they were alike, the
Romans were tried, condemned, and executed in my
eyes.

Nevertheless, the curé persisted in dabbling with
me in Roman history; and I on my side obstinately
refused to take any interest. The men of the Republic did not stir my blood, and the emperors were all
mixed up in my head. The curé would exclaim in
admiration, would become provoked, would argue;
nothing shook my indifference and my own conviction.

For example, in narrating the history of Mucius
Scævola, I ended thus, —

"He burned his right hand to punish himself for
being deceived, which proves that he was a fool."

The curé, who had heard me a moment before with a
satisfied air, started with indignation.

"A fool, Mademoiselle, and why so?"

"Because the loss of his hand could not make
amends for his error," I answered, "since Porsena
was none the less alive, and since a secretary would
do no better."

"True, ma petite; but Porsena was so frightened as
to raise the siege immediately."

"That, Monsieur le Curé, proves only that Porsena
was a coward."

"Even so. Rome was delivered, and thanks to

whom? Thanks to Scævola, thanks to his heroic deed!"

And the curé, who, shuddering at the idea of burning his little finger, only admired Mucius Scævola the more, became enthusiastic and strove to make me appreciate his hero.

"I hold to what I have said," I answered quietly, "that he was only a fool, and a great one."

The curé gasped and exclaimed,—

"When children undertake to argue, mortals hear much foolishness."

"Monsieur le Curé, you told me the other day that the reasoning faculty is the most excellent that man possesses."

"Without doubt, — without doubt, when he knows how to employ it. Then I was speaking of a man grown and not of little girls."

"Monsieur le Curé, the little birds try their wings on the edge of the nest."

The worthy man, a little disconcerted, ran his hands through his hair energetically, which gave him the look of a wolf's head powdered white.

"You do wrong to argue so much, ma petite," he said to me sometimes; "it is a sin of pride. You will not have me always to answer you; and when you are fighting the battle of life, you will learn that one does not argue with it, one submits."

But I do not trouble myself much as to life.   I

have a curé to practise my logic upon, and that is enough for me.

When I had been very teasing, tiring, and tormenting, he would try to assume a severe expression, but he was obliged to give up the attempt; his mouth, always smiling, absolutely refused to obey him.

Then he would say to me,—

"Mademoiselle de Lavalle, you will go over your Roman emperors again, and you will do it in such a way as not to confound Tiberius and Vespasian."

"Let us leave those good people alone, Monsieur le Curé," I would answer; "they tire me. Do you know that if you had lived in their time they would have grilled you alive, or torn out your tongue and nails, or cut you into little pieces like the meat in a pâté?"

At this gloomy picture the curé started slightly, and trotted off without deigning to answer me.

I knew that his displeasure was at its height when he called me Mademoiselle de Lavalle. This ceremonious title was its most active manifestation; and I was filled with remorse until the instant when I saw him appear again, his hair blowing in the wind and a smile on his lips.

CHAPTER II.

M Y aunt treated me harshly when I was a child, and I was so afraid of blows that I obeyed her without a word. She beat me even on my sixteenth birthday, but that was the last time. After that day, so full of events of peculiar interest to me, a revolution, which for some months had been secretly gathering head in me, broke out all at once and changed completely my behaviour toward her.

At that time the curé and I were reviewing the history of France, which I flattered myself I knew very well. Certainly, considering the omissions and the reservations of my book, my knowledge was as complete as possible.

The curé professed a love amounting almost to veneration for her kings, and yet he did not admire Francis I. This antipathy was the more singular, for

Francis I. was valorous, and is still a popular hero. But he did not please the curé, who lost no opportunity to criticise him; consequently, in a spirit of contradiction, I selected him as my favourite.

On the day of which I have spoken above, I was to recite a lesson about my friend. I thought a long time the evening before how I might make him shine in the curé's eyes. Unfortunately I could only quote the words of my history to sustain my views, which were based more on an impression than on actual facts.

I racked my brains for an hour, when a brilliant idea flashed through my head.

"The library!" I exclaimed.

I instantly ran through a long corridor, and entered, for the first time, a room of moderate size lined with shelves covered with books, all firmly bound together by a multitude of spider-webs. It communicated with the rooms which had been closed and never used after my uncle's death, and was so mouldy and close that I was nearly stifled. I made haste to open a tiny window which had neither shutters nor blinds, and gave on the wildest part of the garden; then I proceeded to investigate. But how was I to find Francis I. among all these volumes?

I was about to give the thing up when the title of a little book made me cry out for joy; it was the lives of the kings of France to Henry IV. only. A fair engraving, showing Francis I. in the splendid costume of the Valois, was inserted. I examined it with astonishment.

"Is it possible," I said to myself in amazement, "that there were men as beautiful as that?"

The biographer, who did not share the antipathy of the curé for my hero, praised him without stint. He spoke with an enthusiastic conviction of his beauty, his valour, his chivalrous spirit, and of the enlightened support he extended to letters and the arts. He ended with two lines about his private life, and I learned that of which I was entirely ignorant, — it was this:—

"Francis I. led a joyous life, and loved the ladies dearly. He preferred, above all and sincerely, the lovely Anne de Pisseleu, whom he married to the Comte d'Étampes, whom he had created a duke that he might be more acceptable to her."

From these words I drew the following conclusions: First, having discovered, within the month, that my life was monotonous, that I lacked many things, that the possession of a curé, an aunt, fowls and rabbits, was not enough to create happiness, I decided that, a joyous life being evidently the opposite of mine, Francis I. had shown great judgment in choosing it;

Second, that he certainly practised the holy virtue of charity which my curé preached, since he loved the ladies so much;

2

Third, that Anne de Pisseleu was a fortunate person, and that I should have been much pleased to have a king marry me to a count whom he had created a duke to be "more acceptable" to me.

"Bravo!" I cried, tossing the book up to the ceiling and catching it again skilfully, "here is what will confound the curé, and convert him to my opinion."

That night in bed I re-read the little biography.

"What a gallant man was this Francis I.!" I said to myself. "But why does the author speak of his affection for ladies only? Why does he not say that he loved men too? After all, each one to his taste; but if I may judge women by my aunt, I think that I should have a marked preference for the men."

Then I recalled that the biographer was of the masculine gender; and I concluded that he had thought it polite, amiable, and modest to pass over himself and his fellows in silence.

I went to sleep with this brilliant idea.

The next day I rose in great good-humour. In the first place, I was sixteen years old; besides, the little creature who looked at herself in the glass saw a face that did not displease her; then I made two or three pirouettes as I thought of the stupefaction of the curé before my new learning.

In my impatience I was installed at my table already for some time when he arrived, rosy and smiling. At sight of him my heart beat a little, like those of great captains the night before a battle.

"Come, ma petite," he said, when the exercises were corrected and he had made a face over their brevity, "let us take up Francis I., and examine him from all points of view."

He settled himself comfortably in his chair, took his snuff-box in one hand, his handkerchief in the other, and, looking askance at me, prepared to maintain the argument which he saw was forthcoming.

I entered with great speed upon my subject; I grew earnest; I became excited; I was enthusiastic. I dwelt at length on the qualities extolled in my history, after which I passed to my especial bits of information,—

"And what a charming man, Monsieur le Curé! His figure was majestic, his face noble and beautiful, with such a lovely beard, worn in a point, and such fine eyes!"

I stopped for an instant to take breath, and the curé, looking scared and rising with a start like a Jack-in-a-box, cried, —

"Where have you picked up this stuff, Mademoiselle?"

"That is my secret," I said, with a little mysterious smile.

And burning my ships,—

"Monsieur le Curé, I cannot think what this poor Francis I. has done to you! Do you know that he had great judgment? He led a joyous life and loved the ladies dearly."

Then the eyes of the curé opened so wide that I feared they would leap from their sockets. "*Saint Michel! Saint Barnabé!*" he exclaimed, and let his snuff-box fall with so loud a noise that the cat, stretched in an easy-chair, leaped to the floor with a despairing miaow.

My aunt, who was asleep, awoke with a start and cried,—

"Miserable wretch!"—

addressing me and not the cat in tnis fashion, and without knowing what was in question. But this expression invariably began and ended all her remarks.

I had certainly expected to produce a great effect; none the less, I was taken a little aback by the extraordinary expression on the curé's face.

But I began again at once, unconcernedly,—

"He loved especially a beautiful woman to whom he gave a duchy. Acknowledge, Monsieur le Curé, that he was very good, and that it would have been most delightful to be in the place of Anne de Pisseleu."

"*Sainte Mère de Dieu!*" murmured the curé, in an inaudible voice, "the child is possessed!"

"What is it?" cried my aunt, transfixing her chignon with one of her knitting-needles; "send her out of the room if she is impertinent."

"My child," said the curé, "where did you learn what you have told me?"

"In a book," I answered shortly, without mentioning the library.

"And how could you repeat such abominations?"

"Abominations!" I said, scandalized. "What, Monsieur le Curé, do you find it abominable that Francis I. was generous and loved the ladies? Do you not love them, then, yourself?"

"What does she say?" roared my aunt, who had been listening attentively for some minutes, and who drew from my question the most direful surmises. "Little brazen face, you —"

"Peace, my good woman, peace!" interrupted the curé, appearing all at once relieved of a great weight. "Let me have an explanation with Reine. Let us see; what do you find praiseworthy in the conduct of Francis I.?"

"Truly, it is very simple," I answered in a tone a little contemptuous, thinking that my curé must be growing old and slow of comprehension. "You exhort me every day to love my neighbour; it seems to me that Francis I. put in practice your favourite precept, 'Love your neighbour as yourself, for the love of God.'"

Hardly had I finished my sentence, when the curé, mopping his face, on which rolled great drops of sweat, threw himself back in his chair, and crossing his hands over his stomach, abandoned himself to a

Homeric laugh which lasted so long that tears of
vexation and annoyance came to my eyes.

"Truly," I said in a trembling voice, "I was very
foolish to take so much trouble to learn my lesson,
and to make you admire Francis I."

"My good little child," he said at last, regaining
his serious tone, and using his favourite expression
when he was pleased with me, — "my good little child,
that which caused me so much astonishment was that
I did not know that you felt such an admiration for
those who practised the virtue of charity."

"In any case, it is not a laughing matter," I said in
a sullen tone.

"Come, come, do not let us quarrel."

And the curé, giving me a little pat on the cheek,
cut short the lesson, said that he would return the
next day, and went to confiscate the key of the library,
which he knew of without my suspecting it.

He had not even left the court before my aunt
rushed at me, shaking me hard enough to dislocate
my shoulder.

"Silly wretch, what have you said, what have you
done, to make the curé go so early?"

"If you do not know the reason," I said, "why do
you get angry?"

"Ah! I do not know! Did I not hear what you
said to the curé, brazen face?"

Considering words not sufficient to express her

wrath, she boxed my ears, struck me roughly, and
turned me out of the room like a little dog.

I fled to my room, where I barricaded the door
securely. My first care was to take off my dress, and
to note in the glass that my aunt's thin and bony fingers had left blue marks on my shoulders.

"Wretched little slave," I said, pointing my finger
at my reflection, "how long will you stand such
things? Are you such a coward as not to dare
revolt?"

I admonished myself severely for some minutes;
then, a reaction coming, I threw myself into a chair
and burst into tears.

"What have I done," thought I, "to be treated so?
The wicked woman! And yet why was the curé so
amused while I recited my lesson?"

And I began to laugh, while the tears rolled down
my cheeks. But though I strove hard, I could find
no solution to the problem.

Approaching the open window, I was looking at the
garden in melancholy mood, and was regaining my
self-possession, when I seemed to recognize the voice
of my aunt talking with Suzon. I leaned forward a
little to hear their conversation. ·

"You should be ashamed!" said Suzon; "the little
one is only a child. If you treat her harshly, she will
complain to Monsieur de Pavol, who will take her to
live with him."

"I would like mightily to see it! But how should she ever think of her uncle? It is a chance if she knows of his existence."

"Bah! The child is clever, and a single flash of memory will be enough to send you to the right about, if you make her unhappy; and her good income will disappear with her."

"Ah! well, we shall see. I will not strike her again, but —"

They moved away and I did not hear the end of the sentence.

After dinner, at which I refused to appear, I went to find Suzon.

Suzon had been my aunt's friend before becoming her cook. They quarrelled ten times a day, but were not able to live apart. You will hardly believe me when I say that Suzon loved her mistress sincerely, but that is the exact truth.

But if she forgave my aunt personally her rise on the social ladder, she doubtless cherished a grudge against her fellow-creatures, circumstances, and life, for she never stopped scolding. She had a face bearded like a highwayman, and always wore short petticoats and slippers without heels, though she never went to town to sell the milk, and had no more imagination than Perrette.

"Suzon," I said to her, planting myself before her deliberately, "I am rich, then?"

"Who has told you such stuff, Mademoiselle?"

"That is no affair of yours, Suzon. I wish you to answer me, and to tell me where my Uncle de Pavol lives."

"I wish, I wish!" grumbled Suzon. "She is no longer a child, upon my word. Go about your business, Mademoiselle; I will tell you nothing, because I know nothing."

"You are not telling the truth, Suzon, and I forbid you to answer me so. I heard what you said to my aunt just now."

"Very well, Mademoiselle, if you have heard, it is not necessary for me to take the trouble to tell you."

Suzon turned her back on me and would not answer any of my questions.

J returned to my room, thoroughly exasperated; and, remaining a long time leaning on my elbow at the window, I called the moon, the stars, and the trees to witness that I had formed a firm resolve not to allow myself to be struck, to no longer fear my aunt, and to devote all my wits to making myself disagreeable to her.

And as I dropped the petals of a flower which I was tearing to pieces, I threw to the winds my fears, my pusillanimity, and my timidity of the past. I felt that I was no longer the same person, and I went to sleep comforted.

During the night I dreamed that my aunt, transformed into a dragon, fought with Francis I., who slew her with his great sword. He took me in his arms and flew away with me, while the curé watched us with a melancholy air, and mopped his face with his checked handkerchief. Then he wrung it out with all his might, and the sweat ran from it as if it had been soaked in the river.

CHAPTER III.

THE next morning hardly were we seated at our
table, the curé and I, when the door opened
with a crash and we saw Perrine enter, her bonnet on
her neck and her sabots, stuffed with straw, in her
hand.

"Is the house on fire?" demanded my aunt.

"No, Madame; but the very devil is to pay. The
cow is in the field of barley which is doing so well;
she is destroying it all,—I cannot get her out. The
fowls are on the roof, and the rabbits are in the vegetable-garden."

"In the vegetable-garden!" exclaimed my aunt, who
sprang up, darting an angry glance at me, for the
kitchen-garden was a sacred place to her, and the
object of her only affections.

"My beautiful fowls!" grumbled Suzon, who judged it *à propos* to appear and unite her crabbed note with the shrill one of her mistress.

"Ah, you jade!" cried my aunt.

She hurried out at the heels of the servants, slamming the door angrily.

"Monsieur le Curé," I said at once, "do you believe that in the whole world there is another woman as hateful as my aunt?"

"Well, well! Ma petite, why do you say this?"

"Do you know what she did yesterday, Monsieur le Curé? She beat me!"

"Beat!" repeated the curé, in a tone of incredulity, so impossible did it appear to him that any one would dare to touch, even with the end of a finger, a little creature as delicate as I.

"Yes, beat! and if you do not believe me, I will show you the mark of the blows."

With the word I began to unbutton my dress. The curé looked straight before him with a frightened air.

"It is not necessary! It is not necessary! I believe your word," he cried hastily, his face crimson, and his eyes modestly directed to the tips of his shoes.

"To beat me on my sixteenth birthday!" I went on, re-buttoning my dress. "Do you know, I detest her."

And I struck the table with my fist and hurt myself severely.

"Come, come, my good little child," said the curé, much disturbed, "calm yourself, and tell me what you did."

"Nothing at all! When you left, she called me shameless, and threw herself on me like a fury! The wicked woman!"

"Come, Reine, come, you know that we must forgive our enemies."

"Ah, indeed!" I cried, pushing my chair back suddenly, and striding up and down the salon, "I will never forgive her,—never, never!"

The curé rose too, and began to pace in such fashion that in continuing our conversation we passed each other continually, like the ogre and little Hop o' my Thumb, when he has stolen one of the seven-league boots and the monster is in pursuit.

"You must be reasonable, Reine, and take this humiliation as a kind of penance for the remission of your sins!"

"My sins!" I exclaimed, stopping and shrugging my shoulders slightly; "you know well, Monsieur le Curé, that they are so small, so small, that they are not worth mentioning."

"Indeed!" said the curé, who was not able to keep back a smile. "Then, since you are a saint, bear your troubles patiently for the love of God."

"Not I," I answered in a very decided tone; "I am perfectly willing to love the good God a little, —not too much; do not frown, Monsieur le Curé, — but I understand that he loves me enough not to be at all pleased at seeing me unhappy."

"What a head!" exclaimed the curé. "What an education I have given her!"

"In short," I continued, beginning to pace again, "I wish revenge, and I will have it."

"Reine, this is very wrong. Be silent and hear me."

"Revenge is the delight of the gods," I answered, jumping up to catch a big fly that was hovering over my head.

"Let us speak seriously, ma petite."

"But I am speaking seriously," I answered, stopping an instant before a glass to note, with some satisfaction, that animation was very becoming to me. "You will see, Monsieur le Curé, I will take a sword, and I will decapitate my aunt as Judith did Holofernes."

"The child is mad!" cried the curé, with a distressed air. "Calm yourself, Mademoiselle, and do not talk foolishness."

"Very well, Monsieur le Curé; but confess that Judith was not worth two sous."

The curé leaned back against the mantel-piece and delicately took a pinch of snuff.

"Pardon me, ma petite, that depends on the point of view from which one observes her."

"How illogical you are!" I said. "You think Judith's action superb because she delivered some paltry Jews, who were certainly not worth as much as I, and who ought not to interest you at all, since they have been dead and buried this long time; and you think it very wrong that I should do as much for my own deliverance. And Heaven knows that I am very much alive," I added, spinning around many times on my heels.

"You have a good opinion of yourself," answered the curé, forcing himself to assume a severe air.

"Ah, excellent!"

"Come, will you listen to me now?"

"I am sure," I said, pursuing my idea, "that Holofernes was infinitely more agreeable than my aunt, and that I should have got on with him perfectly. Consequently, I cannot see any great objection to my imitating Judith."

"Reine!" cried the curé, stamping his foot.

"My dear curé, do not be angry, I beg. You can reassure yourself; I shall not kill my aunt,— I have another way to take my revenge."

"Tell it to me," said the excellent man, softened at once, as he fell into a chair.

I seated myself beside him.

"Very well. You have heard of my Uncle de Pavol?"

"Certainly. He lives near V——."

"Excellent! What is the name of his estate?"

"Pavol."

"Then if I wrote to my uncle at the Château Pavol near V——, the letter would arrive safely?"

"Without doubt."

"Then, Monsieur le Curé, I have found my revenge. You know that though my aunt does not love me, she loves my money."

"But, my child," said the curé, astounded, "where did you learn this?"

"I heard her say it herself, so I am sure of what I state. She fears above all that I will complain to Monsieur de Pavol, and that I will ask him to take me to live with him. I count on threatening to write to my uncle; and I do not say," I continued after a moment's hesitation, "that I shall not do it, some day or other."

"Come, that is harmless enough," said the good curé, smiling.

"You will see," I cried, clapping my hands; "do you approve?"

"Yes, up to a certain point, ma petite, for it is clear that you should not be struck; but I forbid any impertinence. Do not use your weapon except for legitimate defence, and remember that if your aunt has faults, you owe her respect and should not be , in the least aggressive."

I made an expressive grimace.

"I promise you nothing; or rather, wait, — to be

frank, I promise to do exactly the opposite of what you say."

"It is a veritable revolt! I shall end by being angry, Reine."

"It is more than a revolt," I replied gravely; "it is a revolution."

"I am at the end of my patience and my wits," muttered the curé. "Mademoiselle de Lavalle, be so good as to submit to my authority."

"Listen," I went on in a coaxing tone; "I love you with all my heart. You are indeed the only person in the world that I do love."

The curé's face brightened.

"But I detest, I execrate my aunt; my opinions on this subject will never change. I am much more intelligent than she —"

Here the curé, whose face was growing dark, broke in with a hasty exclamation.

"Do not protest," I went on, watching him slyly: "you know that you are of my opinion."

"What an education! what an education!" murmured the curé, in a piteous tone.

"Monsieur le Curé, my salvation is not jeopardized. Do not disturb yourself. I shall meet you some day or other in heaven," I resumed. "Having, then, much more intelligence than my aunt, it will be easy to irritate her by my remarks. Last night I swore to

myself to be very disagreeable. I called the moon
and stars to witness my oath."

"My child," said the curé, "you are not willing to
hear me, and you will be sorry."

"Bah! We shall see about that! I hear my aunt;
she is furious because it was I who let out the cow,
the fowls, and rabbits, in order to be alone with you.
Give her a talking to, Monsieur le Curé. I assure you
that she struck me very hard; I have black marks on
my shoulders."

My aunt entered like a hurricane, and the stunned
curé had no time to answer me.

"Reine, come here!" she cried, her face purple with
rage and the hurried chase she had had after the rabbits.

I made her a deep courtesy.

"I leave you with the curé," I said, darting a look
of intelligence at my ally.

The window, most fortunately, was open.

I jumped into a chair, threw my legs over the sill,
and let myself drop into the garden, to the great astonishment of my aunt, who had stationed herself before
the door to cut off my retreat.

I confess that I pretended to run away, but that in
reality I hid behind a laurel and had such delight as
never before in hearing the reproaches of the curé and
the furious exclamations of my aunt. That evening,
during dinner, she had the pleasant manners of a
mastiff from whom one has taken a bone.

She scolded Suzon, who bade her mind her business, maltreated her cat, and threw the silver on the table with a horrible noise; finally, exasperated at my impassible and satirical air, she seized a carafe, and threw it out of the window.

I instantly seized a dish of rice, which she had not yet tasted, and sent it after the carafe.

"Miserable fool!" shouted my aunt, darting toward me.

"Do not come near me," I said, retreating; "if you touch me, I will write to my Uncle de Pavol."

"Ah!" exclaimed my aunt, standing petrified, her arm raised.

"If not to-night," I added, "to-morrow, or in a day or two, for I do not propose to be beaten."

"Your uncle will not believe you," cried my aunt.

"Oh, yes, indeed. Your fingers have left their mark on my shoulders. I know that he is very kind, and I will go to him."

I had really no knowledge of my uncle's character, as I was six years old when I saw him for the first and last time. But I thought that I ought to appear to have known about him for a long time, and that by so doing I should show great diplomacy. I went out majestically, leaving my aunt to overflow into the breast of Suzon.

CHAPTER IV.

WAR was declared; and from that moment I passed my time in fighting Madame de Lavalle. Until then I had hardly dared to open my mouth before her, unless the curé made a third; for she would bid me be silent even before I had finished my sentence.

I assure you that this method of procedure was particularly disagreeable to me, because I am extremely fond of talking. I made up for it a little with the curé, but this was entirely insufficient. I had, besides, acquired the habit of talking aloud to myself. I often took my stand before my mirror and talked to my reflection for whole hours.

My dear mirror! faithful friend! confidant of my most secret thoughts!

I do not know whether men have ever considered seriously the enormous influence which this little piece of furniture can exercise on the mind. Note that I do not specify the sex of the mind, being perfectly convinced that individuals with beards have as much pleasure in observing their appearance as we.

If I were writing a philosophic work, I should select as my subject, The Influence of the Mirror on the Intellect and Heart of Mankind.

I do not deny that my treatise would perhaps be unique of its kind, that it would in no way resemble the philosophy in which Kant, Fichte, Schelling, and others have dabbled all their lives, to their own great glory, and the still greater happiness of posterity, which reads them with an interest the more keen that it understands nothing. No; my treatise will not follow at all in the footsteps of these gentlemen. It will be clear, concise, practical, with a touch of the caustic; and one must push the love of contradiction very far not to admit that these characteristics do not appertain to the philosophies above mentioned. But not finding my knowledge sufficiently ripe for this great work, I content myself with cherishing for my mirror a sincere affection, and with looking at myself every day for a long time in a spirit of thankfulness.

I am perfectly aware that in face of this revelation

some of those peevish, fault-finding spirits who see everything at its darkest will insinuate that coquetry plays a great part in the feeling which I profess for my mirror. *Mon Dieu!* one is not perfection, and note, good reader, that if you are sincere, which is by no means certain, you will acknowledge that personal interest, to use no harsher word, holds first place in the greater part of your opinions.

To return to my subject, I will say that, having broken entirely with my old fears, I no longer tried to restrain my loquacity before my aunt. There was not a meal when we did not have discussions that threatened to degenerate into tempests.

Although I did not yet know her origin, I was not slow to discover that she was as ignorant as a carp, and that she experienced a lively vexation when I supported my opinions by my knowledge or that of the curé, — though as to that, I never hesitated to give the authority of history to ideas drawn from my own brain. Unfortunately it was not possible for me to combat the personal experience of my aunt; and when she asserted that things were thus and so in the world, that men were nothing at all but scamps and tools of Satan, I was angry because I could make no reply. I had enough good sense to perceive that the persons with whom I was living could give me a most imperfect idea of human kind in the ordinary circumstances of life.

The curé dined with us every Sunday. He had, doubtless, his private reasons for not crying up the lords of creation before me, — except when it concerned his heroes of antiquity, on behalf of whom he had no longer to fear an enterprising spirit, — because he offered the weakest denials to the assertions of my aunt.

The Sunday dinner was composed invariably of a capon or a fowl, a salad of hard-boiled eggs, and curds, if it were the season. The curé, whose cheer was of the slightest at home, and whose palate could appreciate Suzon's cooking, used to arrive rubbing his hands, and declaring himself famished.

We placed ourselves at the table immediately, and the beginning of the conversation was as invariable as the menu.

"It is beautiful weather," my aunt would say. Her remark, if it rained, was varied only by a change of the adjective.

"Superb weather," the curé would answer joyously. "It is delightful to walk in the bright sunshine."

If it had rained, if it had snowed, if it had frozen, if it had hailed stones and brimstone, the curé would have expressed his satisfaction as strongly as if expatiating on the charms of a snug room or singing the praises of a blazing fire.

"But it is not cold," my aunt would add. "It is astonishing. In my time we put on white dresses at Easter."

"Were white dresses becoming to you?" I would ask eagerly.

My aunt, who foresaw some impertinence, launched a forbidding look at me before replying,—

"Certainly, very becoming."

"Oh!" I would exclaim, in a tone which left no doubt as to my private opinion.

"In my time," my aunt would say, "little girls did not speak unless they were spoken to."

"You never spoke when you were young, Aunt?"

"When some one spoke to me, not otherwise."

"And were all the girls like you, Aunt?"

"Certainly, my niece."

"What a horrible time!" I would sigh, raising my eyes to heaven.

The curé would look at me reproachfully, and Madame de Lavalle would eye the different objects on the table, evidently greatly tempted to throw something at my head.

Conversation, having reached this acute stage, would cease suddenly, until my aunt's sharp humours, held in check by an effort of will, exploded all at once like a boiler subjected to too strong pressure. She would vent her wrath upon all creation. Men, women, and children,—nothing escaped it. Of the poor men there was left at the dinner's end only a horrible mixture, not of bones and mangled flesh, but of monsters of all kinds.

"Men are not worth a dog's trotters," my aunt would say, in the harmonious and choice language which was habitual to her.

The curé, who realized the unfortunate fact that he was not a woman, lowered his head and appeared full of contrition.

"What miscreants! what scamps!" my aunt would go on, regarding me with a furious look, as if I belonged to the class in question.

"Humph!" the curé would say.

"Creatures who think of nothing but to enjoy themselves and eat," she would add, smarting under the poverty bequeathed her by her husband. "What tools of Satan!"

"Humph! humph!" the curé would say again, nodding his head.

"Monsieur le Curé," I would cry impatiently, "'humph' is not a very strong argument."

"Allow me,—allow me," the worthy man would say, disturbed in the enjoyment of his dinner. "I think that Madame de Lavalle said more than she really meant in using the expression 'tools of Satan.' But it is true that there are many men who do not inspire much confidence."

"You are like Francis I.,—you prefer the ladies," I would say, with my little candid air.

"*Palsambleu!*" my aunt would cry. She had replaced certain most expressive words of her own with this one, borrowed from her husband, which seemed to her thoroughly aristocratic,—"*Palsambleu!* hold your tongue, fool!"

But the curé would make a mysterious sign, and the excellent woman would bite her lips.

"And your heroes, Monsieur le Curé, your Greeks and Romans?"

"Oh, the men of to-day are not in the least like those of antiquity," the curé would say, entirely certain that he expressed a great truth.

"And the curés?" I would ask.

"The curés are not under consideration," he would answer with a pleasant smile.

This kind of conversation, filled with hidden meanings, had the effect of stimulating me tremendously. I became aware that a world of ideas and sentiments was unknown to me, and that I ought to lose no time in discovering it. I had my doubts as to the absolute justice of my aunt's condemnation of humanity; but I understood that I was ignorant of many things, and that I was likely to remain a long time in my ignorance.

One morning when I was meditating on this lamentable state of affairs, the idea occurred to me to consult the three persons whom I was able to see every day: Jean the farmer, Perrine, and Suzon.

The last-named having lived at C——, I decided that her estimate ought to be based on a wide experience, and I reserved her for a *bonne bouche*.

Wrapping myself in a cloak, I took my sabots and the road to the farm, which was about a half-mile from the house.

Paddling, splashing, plunging, I reached Jean, who was cleaning his plough.

"Good-morning, Jean."

"Good-morning, Mamselle," said Jean, taking off his worsted hat; whereupon all his hair stood up straight on his head. When it was not under pressure, it was given to indulging in this little practice.

"I come to consult you on a subject very, very important," I said, emphasizing the adverb to awaken his wits, which I knew were disposed to be wool gathering when he was questioned.

"At your service, Mamselle."

"My aunt says that all men are scamps; what is your opinion on the subject, Jean?"

"Scamps!" repeated Jean, opening his eyes as if he perceived a monster before him.

"Yes; but that is my aunt's opinion, and I wish yours."

"*Dame!* it ought to be the same."

"But that is not an opinion, Jean. Come, do you believe, yes or no, that men are generally scamps?"

Jean laid the first finger of his right hand on the end of his nose, which is, as every one is aware, the evidence of profound thought.

After having reflected a good minute, he made me this clear and decisive answer, —

"Listen, Mamselle; I will tell you. It may be yes, but then it may be no."

"Blockhead!" I exclaimed, indignant at contemplating such phenomenal stupidity.

He opened his eyes; he opened his mouth; he opened his hands; he would have opened his entire person if he had been able, to show his astonishment better.

I returned to the courtyard of Buisson, storming at the mud, my sabots, Jean, and myself.

"Perrine," I cried, "come here."

Perrine, who was cleaning her milk-pans, ran at once, a bunch of nettles in her hand, her arms bare, her face red as a lady apple, and her bonnet on the back of her head, as was her habit.

"What is your opinion about men?" I asked abruptly.

"About men!"

And Perrine changed from the red of an apple to that of a peony, dropped her nettles, seized the corner of her apron, lifted her left foot and remained perched on the right, while she looked at me with amazement.

"Well, then, answer! What do you think of men?"

"Mamselle is making fun of me, surely!"

"Not at all; I am speaking seriously. Answer quickly."

"*Dame!* Mamselle," said Perrine, standing erect again on her two legs, "when they are handsome lads my opinion is that there are worse things to look at."

This way of considering the question gave me great matter for reflection.

"I am not speaking of their personal appearance," I said, shrugging my shoulders, "but of their character."

"*Ma foi!* I have found them most amiable," answered Perrine, whose little eyes sparkled.

"What! you have not found them miscreants, scamps, tools of Satan?"

Perrine burst into a broad laugh.

"You see, Mamselle, the talk of these miscreants is so pleasant that — "

Here she broke off and gave her head a great thump with her fist. She twisted her apron, dropped her eyes, and seemed disposed to take to her heels.

"What next? finish your sentence!"

"Mamselle makes me talk nonsense,—that is certain. I am going."

And making me her best courtesy, she disappeared in the depths of the dairy, shutting the door in my face.

Why did she say nonsense? Come, Suzon is my last resource; it remains to be seen if she will speak.

I went into the kitchen. Suzon, armed with a broom, was preparing for active work. It seemed to me that she had one of her blue days, and I judged that it would be judicious to use some oratorical skill in propounding my question.

"How beautiful your coppers are, and how they shine!" I said graciously.

"I do the best I can," grumbled Suzon. "After all, those who don't like it have only to say so."

"Your fricassee of fowl is a great success, Suzon," I continued, undiscouraged; "you must teach me how to make it."

"It is not proper work for you, Mademoiselle; stay in your own part of the house and leave me in peace in my kitchen."

My methods of conciliation not producing any effect, I turned my batteries in another direction.

"Do you know one thing, Suzon? You must have been very pretty when you were young," I said, thinking to myself that if I had been her husband I would have put her to bake in the oven to get rid of her.

I had touched a responsive chord, for Suzon deigned to smile.

"Every one was pretty once, Mademoiselle."

"Suzon," I resumed, profiting by this sudden softening to get more quickly to my subject, "I want to ask one question. What is your opinion of men — and women?" I added, thinking it ingenious to extend my studies to both sexes.

Suzon leaned on her broom, assumed her most severe expression, and answered me with absolute conviction,—

"Women, Mademoiselle, are not much, but men are nothing at all."

"Oh!" I protested; "are you sure?"

"As sure as that I speak to you, Mademoiselle."

She gave a great blow with her broom to the parings of vegetables that were on the floor, and made them disappear with as much dexterity as if they represented the bipeds so obnoxious to her.

I retired to my room to meditate on the misanthropic axiom of Suzon, discouraged enough to think that I was not much, and that my unknown friends, the men, merited the humiliating description of being nothing at all.

CHAPTER V.

NEVERTHELESS, my studies of morals appearing to me totally inadequate, I resolved to continue them with the aid of the romances in the library.

Regularly on a Monday, the day of the fair, my aunt, the curé, and Suzon went together to C——. My aunt had decided, as she always did, that I should remain under the charge of Perrine, and for the first time in my life, I was enchanted at this decision. I was sure to be left to my own devices, Perrine busying herself far more with her cow than with my doings.

For an excursion such as this the farmer, at eight
o'clock in the morning, brought into the courtyard a
sort of tilted cart, called in those parts a *maringote*.
My aunt appeared in her best clothes, her head adorned
with a round hat of black felt, to which she had fastened strings of tender violet. She placed it jauntily
on the top of her chignon. She was wrapped in furs,
whether it was warm or cold, having since her marriage adopted the belief that a lady of quality should
never travel without carrying upon her the skin of
some animal. When she was thus arrayed, she firmly
believed that the evidences of her origin were effaced.

She seated herself at the back of the *maringote* on a
chair, upon which was placed a pillow, in order that
that delicate part of the person which a modest pen
refuses to name might not be injured.

Suzon, who was to drive a horse who drove himself,
placed herself on the right of the seat before her, and
the curé climbed up by her side.

Then, as one man, they turned to me.

"Don't do anything foolish," said my aunt, "and
don't go into the kitchen-garden."

"Don't make a mess in my kitchen," said Suzon,
"and be satisfied with cold veal for breakfast."

The curé did not say a word, but he smiled at me
pleasantly, and made a gesture as if to say,—

"I would have liked very much to take you, but
she would not."

On this memorable Monday all went as usual. I took a few steps along the road and saw them disappear, shaking, all three, like salad-baskets.

Without losing an instant, I put into execution a plan which had been ripening for a long time. It was no other than to take possession of the library, whose key the curé had had the unlucky idea of carrying off, but I was not the girl to be discouraged by such a trifle.

I ran to get a ladder, which I dragged under the library window; after superhuman efforts I succeeded in raising it, and planting it solidly against the wall. Clambering quickly up the rounds, I broke a pane of glass with a stone with which I had armed myself: then taking out the pieces of glass sticking to the sash, I passed the upper part of my body through the opening, and dropped into the library.

I fell head-first on the floor, and made a huge bump on my forehead; and the curé, the next day, brought me an ointment for it.

My first care, when I had picked myself up, and the dizziness caused by my fall had passed off, was to rummage the drawers of an old bureau for a key like the one the curé had carried off. My search was not long, and after one or two unsuccessful attempts I found what I wanted.

After having concealed as far as possible the evidences of my house-breaking, I settled myself in a

chair, and while I rested from my exertions, my eye was caught by the works of Walter Scott on a shelf in front of me.   I chose one at random from the set, and went to my room, carrying, as if it were a treasure, "The Fair Maid of Perth."

In all my life I had never read a romance, and I fell into an ecstasy, a rapture, which cannot be expressed. Should I live nine hundred and sixty-nine years, like the good Methuselah, I shall never forget my impressions on reading "The Fair Maid of Perth."

I felt the joy of a prisoner transported from his cell into the midst of trees, flowers, and sunshine, or better still, of an artist who hears played for the first time, and to perfection, the work of his heart and brain. That unknown world, for which I was unconsciously sighing, was opened to me all at once.   A light shone suddenly into my brain, which I had thought until then dull and idiotic.   I was intoxicated, inebriated, by this romance, so full of colour, life, and movement.

That evening I went, as in a dream, down to the dining-room, where the curé, who was to take dinner with us, was impatiently awaiting me.

He looked at my face with deep sympathy, and asked, with the greatest interest, how the accident had happened.

"An accident?" I said with astonishment.

"Your forehead is all black and blue, ma petite Reine."

"The blockhead has been climbing up a tree or a ladder," said my aunt.

"A ladder; yes, you are right," I answered.

"My poor child!" cried the curé; "you fell on your head?"

I made a sign of assent.

"Have you used arnica, ma petite?"

"Bah! it serves her right," said my aunt. "Eat your soup, Monsieur le Curé, and do not trouble about this giddy pate. She got no more than she deserves."

The curé said no more, but made a little friendly sign, and watched me stealthily.

But I did not pay much attention to what went on around me. I was thinking of that charming Catherine Glover, and that brave Henry Smith, with whom I had fallen in love until some one better should come along, — when, behold, without the slightest warning I broke into sobs.

"Ah, *mon Dieu!*" cried the curé, springing up. "My dear little Reine! my good little child!"

"Leave her alone," said my aunt; "she is sulky because she did not go with us to C——."

But the curé, who knew that I detested tears, and that I was too proud to show before my aunt any mortification of which she was the cause, came to me, and asked in a low tone why I cried, and tried to comfort me.

"There is nothing the matter, my dear, good curé," I said, drying my tears and trying to smile. "You see I have a horror of pain, my head aches, and then I must be a spectacle."

"No more than usual," said my aunt.

The curé looked at me uneasily. He was not satisfied with my explanation, and said to himself that something out of the common had happened during the day. He advised me to go to bed without delay, which I did straightway.

I was mortified at having made an exhibition of feeling, and all the more mortified that I did not know why I had cried. Was it from pleasure or vexation? I could not tell, and I went to sleep saying to myself that it was useless to try to analyze my feeling.

During the following month I devoured the greater part of Walter Scott's works. Truly, since then I have had deep and real joys; but however great they have been, I do not know that they have been more keen than those I experienced when my mind emerged from its mist, like a butterfly from its chrysalis. I went from rapture to rapture, from ecstasy to ecstasy. I thought of nothing but my romances and the characters that excited my imagination.

When the curé explained to me a problem, I thought of Rebecca, whom I had left *tête-à-tête* with the Templar; when he gave me a course of history, I saw march before me those delightful heroes, among whom my fickle heart had already chosen more than a dozen husbands; when he reproached me, I did not hear more than half, being engaged in designing a costume like that of Queen Elizabeth or Amy Robsart.

"What have you done to-day?" he would ask on arriving.

"Nothing."

"How nothing?"

"All this wearies me," I would say with a tired air.

The poor curé was in dismay. He concocted long exordiums, and delivered them at me without stopping for breath; but he would have produced as much effect had he addressed a redskin.

Presently I became all at once very depressed. If my aunt no longer struck me, she made up for it by saying disagreeable things. She had discovered that I was mortified at being so small. She never lost an opportunity to wound me in this vulnerable spot; she called me a shrimp, and kept reiterating that I was ugly.

Not long before, I had thought myself very pretty, and had much more confidence in my opinion than in my aunt's. But in making acquaintance with Walter Scott's heroines, a misgiving arose in my mind. They were so beautiful that I was wretched at the thought that one must be like them to be loved.

The curé, through very sympathy, lost his smiles and his colour. He watched me with a tearful look, spent his time in taking snuff, forgetting all the etiquette of the art, and tried to discover my secret, employing Machiavellian means to gain his ends, but I was impenetrable.

One day I saw him go toward the library, but I had been careful not to leave the key in the lock; he came back shaking his head, and running his hands through his hair, which, more disordered than ever, looked like a plume.

I was hidden behind a door, and when he passed near me, I heard him mutter,—

"I will come back with the key."

This decision annoyed me greatly. I said to myself that he would surely discover my secret, and that I should not be able to continue my beloved reading.

I went at once to get some volumes, which I took to my room, replacing them on the shelves by books taken at random, but, despite my precautions, I felt sure that the square of paper with which I had replaced the broken pane would cry aloud against me.

It was on that day, while examining some letters which I found in the bureau, I discovered my aunt's origin. It gave me a weapon against her which I resolved not to delay in using.

The next morning at breakfast she was in a bad humour. When she was in that state of mind, if she

could not find a pretext for being disagreeable to me,
she did not wait for it.

I was dreaming of that charming Buckingham, who
seemed to me adorable with his insolence, his fine
clothes, his bows, and his wit, and I was asking myself why Alice Bridgenorth was in despair at finding
herself at his house, when my aunt said to me without
preamble,—

"How ugly you are this morning, Reine!"

I started in my seat.

"Here it is," I said, handing her the salt.

"I did not ask for the salt, idiot.   Truly, you have
become as stupid as you are ugly!"

It is to be noted that my aunt never addressed me
affectionately.   From the day that she became my
uncle's wife, she believed it due to the dignity of her
position to suppress any affectionate expressions.   She
spoke to me as she did to her rabbits.

"I do not share your opinion," I answered dryly; "I
think myself very pretty."

"A good joke!" exclaimed my aunt.   "Pretty! you!
a little shrimp not higher than the mantel-piece!"

"It is better to be like a delicate plant than to just
miss being a man," I answered.

My aunt firmly believed that she had been a beauty,
and would not tolerate jesting on that subject.

"I was beautiful, Mademoiselle, so beautiful that
they called my sister and me goddesses!"

"Did your sister look like you, Aunt?"

"Very much; we were twins."

"Her husband ought to have been a happy man," I said impressively.

My aunt uttered a bad word, which I will not allow my pen to repeat.

"As to that," I resumed calmly, "you have naturally the tastes of a woman of the people, while I,— I —"

But I stopped open-mouthed in the midst of my sentence; my aunt had smashed her plate with the handle of her knife. What I had said showed that all the efforts she had hitherto made to conceal her birth from me had been of no avail, and revenged me in full for all her unkindness.

"You are a serpent!" she cried in a choked voice.

"I think not, Aunt."

"A serpent!"

"You have said that already," I answered, tranquilly swallowing my last strawberry.

"A serpent warmed in my bosom!" repeated my aunt, too angry to draw further on her imagination.

I shook my head, saying to myself that if I were a serpent, I should certainly decline to assume that position of my own free will.

"Permit me," I resumed; "I have studied this animal in my natural history, and I have never seen that it had the habit of being warmed in the bosom of any one whatsoever."

My aunt, always disconcerted when I referred to my reading, made no answer, but the expression of her face seemed to me so little reassuring that I made haste to be off, singing at the top of my voice, "Il était une fois un oncle de Pavol, de Pavol, de Pavol."

We were at the middle of June. Butterflies were flying everywhere; flies were buzzing; the air was full of a thousand odours,— in short, the weather was so charming that I forgot my usual prudence. I took my book, and settled myself in a meadow in the shadow of a haystack.

My heart was a little heavy as I thought of what my aunt had said. It is certainly most distressing to be so small, so very small. Who would ever fall in love with me? But I comforted myself by reading "Peveril of the Peak." Among all Scott's novels this was my first choice, precisely because of Fenella, whose figure was certainly smaller than mine.

I loved, I adored, Buckingham. I was in a rage at Fenella, who said to him things that were really very severe, and at the moment when she disappeared through the window, I stopped reading to exclaim:

"Little simpleton! such a charming man!"

As I uttered the words, I raised my eyes, and gave a loud cry, for there was the curé, standing before me. With folded arms he looked at me in astonishment. He seemed as dismayed as the individual in fairy stories who finds his diamonds changed to nuts.

I rose a little shamefacedly, because I had been abominably entrapped.

"Oh, Reine!" he began.

"My dear curé," I cried, pressing "Peveril of the Peak" to my heart, "I beg you, I pray you, let me keep on!"

"Reine! my little Reine! I never would have believed it of you."

This gentleness softened me, the more that my conscience was not entirely clear; so I set myself to lead him from the subject by tactics peculiarly feminine.

"It was a distraction, Monsieur le Curé, and I am so unhappy."

"Unhappy, Reine?"

"Do you think it can be amusing to have an aunt like mine? She does not beat me any more, it is true; but she says things which give me so much pain."

How well I understood my curé! He had already forgotten his displeasure and his reproaches, the more that there was a solid foundation of truth to my words.

"Is that the reason you are so depressed, my good little child?"

"Certainly, Monsieur le Curé. Consider that my aunt tells me in every possible way that I am a shrimp, and that I am ugly enough to frighten one."

My eyes filled with tears, for the subject was one that went right to my heart.

The good curé, very much disturbed, rubbed his nose with a perplexed air. He was far from sharing my aunt's ideas on this point, and was considering how he might remove my mortification without awakening in my soul pride, vanity, and the other concomitants of damnation.

"Come, Reine, we must not attach too much importance to things which perish so quickly."

"Meanwhile, they exist at the present moment," I replied; thus being in accord, after an interval of two centuries, with the thought of the most beautiful daughter of France.

"And then, you see, perhaps there are people who do not think as Madame de Lavalle."

"Are you one of them, Monsieur le Curé? Do you think me pretty?"

"Ye-es," answered the curé, in a tone of commiseration.

"Very pretty?"

"But — but — yes," answered the curé, in the same tone.

"Ah, how happy I am!" I cried, pirouetting. "How I love you, my dear curé!"

"This is all very well, Reine, but you have committed a serious fault. You have forced your way into the library at the risk of breaking your neck, and you have read books which I should probably never have given you."

"Walter Scott, Monsieur le Curé, only Walter Scott. My literature speaks very highly of him."

And I described to him all my impressions. I talked volubly for a long time, charmed to see that the curé not only had no intention of scolding me, but that he listened with interest to what I was saying. At the sight of my enthusiasm and my cheerfulness, regained as if by magic, he recovered his colour and his smiling looks.

"Come," he said to me, "I will allow you to continue to read Walter Scott, I will even re-read him myself so that I may discuss him with you, but promise me that you will not renew your escapade."

I gave him the promise joyfully, and from that time we had a new subject of discussion and dispute, for, be it understood, we were never of the same mind.

But soon the interest which I felt for my romances was effaced by a surprising, an unheard-of event, which took place some weeks later at Buisson. It was one of those events which do not make empires tremble to their base, but which fill the heart or the imagination of young girls with disturbing thoughts.

CHAPTER VI.

I T was a Sunday.

On Sunday we regularly attended High Mass, which was the only morning service, the curé having no *vicaire*. My aunt entered our armorial pew first; I followed her; Suzon came next; and Perrine closed the file.

Our little church was old and wretched. The original colour of the walls had disappeared under a sort of green slime, caused by the dampness; and the floor, instead of being level, had many fissures and hillocks which invited the faithful to break their necks, and take advantage of being in a sacred place to rise the sooner to the skies. The altar was decorated with figures of angels, painted by the village wheelwright, who prided himself on being an artist; two or three saints surveyed themselves with surprise, astonished at their own ugliness. Often, in looking at them, I have said to myself that if I were a saint, and mortals represented me in so hideous a fashion, I should be absolutely deaf to their prayers; but perhaps the saints have not my temperament. Through a broken window a white rose lifted its perfumed head, and by its beauty and freshness seemed to protest against the bad taste of men.

We were the owners of a harmonium of which only three notes sounded; sometimes the number rose to five, the instrument, owing to the weather, being subject to caprices, like the rheumatism of our precentor, who roared for two hours in so naïve and so profound a belief that he had a fine voice that it was impossible to be out of patience with him.

The *tabouret* of the officiant was placed at the foot of a chasm, in such a way that from my position I could see only the head and shoulders of the curé, who had the appearance of undergoing punishment. The choir-boys made faces and whispered behind his back, without its occurring to him to be annoyed.

After the Gospels he took off his chasuble and stole before us,— it was all in the family,— tripped over some holes, and reached the pulpit.

Among the men and women who live and struggle the wide world over, I suppose there is not one who, at some time in his life, has not had an aspiration. Man, be his position low or high, cannot live without

longings; and the curé, obeying the common law, had
for thirty years of his life dreamed of having a pulpit.

Unhappily, he was very poor; his parishioners were
equally so; and my aunt, who was the only person who
could help him, made no response to his timid hints.
Besides being niggardly in the matter of giving, she
had the very slightest consideration for the curé's
aspiration.

At last, by dint of economy, the curé found himself
one day the master of two hundred francs.   He resolved then to realize his dream, for good or evil.

One morning I saw him arrive, out of breath.

"Ma petite Reine, come with me!" he cried.

"Where, Monsieur le Curé?"

"To the church, come quick!"

"But Mass is over!"

"Yes, yes; but I have something charming to show
you!"

He had such a joyous air, his kindly figure breathed
such lightheartedness, that I laugh now when I think
of it, and his delight is one of my most cherished
memories of those days.

He did not walk, he flew; and we reached the
church on a run.   Men had come to set up the pulpit;
and the curé, in an ecstasy before it, said to me in a
low tone,—

"Look, petite Reine, look! Is it not a happy con-
trivance? At last we have a pulpit! It has not a very

solid look, but it is firm enough. And now the dream of my life is realized! One must never despair of anything, ma petite, never!"

I looked at it a little dismayed, because I could not conceal from myself that my fancy had always pictured a pulpit as something grand, monumental. The one before my eyes was a sort of box of white wood placed on iron supports, and raised so little that in case of necessity one could have entered it without steps. But a pulpit without steps,— such a thing was never seen; so to save its reputation, they had managed to place two, each six inches high.

"See, Reine," said the curé, "what a good effect it produces. When I have a little money, I will have it given a coat of paint, or rather I will paint it myself; that will amuse me, and besides it will be cheaper. It really ought to be a little higher, but one must not be too ambitious."

And the poor, excellent man walked around the pulpit with an admiring air. Had the panels been painted by Raphael or carved by Michael Angelo, he could not have been more happy.

He did not consider that the reality, as, alas! always, did not in the least resemble his dream; he made no comparisons, and enjoyed his happiness without reservation.

"It was I who designed it, my dear child; and it was really a very clever idea. Nevertheless, there is another side to the picture, and I must acknowledge that I am a little in debt; the price asked me is a little higher than I had expected; but it seems that that is always the case when one builds. I counted on buying a great-coat this winter; eh, well! I must go without it, that's all!"

Oh, yes, his joy is one of my sweetest memories of those days. I have never seen a man so happy, and one who so brightened a common pleasure by the reflection of his own kindly disposition, and his almost childish interest.

"It certainly has all the appearance of a pulpit," he said, laughing and rubbing his hands.

I had truly some doubts on this point, but I concealed them, and was as enthusiastic as I could be over this extraordinary object, which, on account of the irregular form of the church, was placed in a recess, so that when the curé preached, three fourths of the congregation saw only an arm and a bit of white hair which moved eloquently in the different stages of the discourse.

The curé was so pleased to say to himself, "I will enter the pulpit," that we had to resign ourselves to having a sermon every Sunday.

Hardly had he opened his mouth than the women made themselves comfortable for a little nap; than Perrine profited by the general drowsiness to ogle the pew next ours; and than Reine de Lavalle set herself to meditate on the vicissitudes of a life represented by an aunt and the vexation of sermons.

I know not why the curé loved to discourse on human passions, but one day when he allowed himself to be carried away in the heat of improvisation, I asked him at dinner questions so indiscreet and embarrassing that he made a firm resolve never again to touch on certain subjects before me. He contented himself thereafter with speaking of idleness, drunkenness, anger, and other vices which excited neither my curiosity nor my loquacity.

For an hour he would lay bare to our eyes the great iniquity in which we were sunk; then, when our moral state had become truly and entirely lamentable, with a radiant air he would descend with us into hell within an inch of the punishments which our sin-ravaged souls deserved; after which, passing by a bold flight of rhetoric to ideas less horrible, he would emerge little by little from the infernal regions, remain a few moments on the earth, and finally leave us happy in heaven, and would descend from his pulpit with the triumphant step of a conqueror who has cut some Gordian knot.

The congregation would wake up with a start, except Suzon, who was too happy to hear evil of humanity to sleep, and who drank it all in while the curé whipped his flock with his flowers of rhetoric.

It was, then, a Sunday. The heat was overpower-
ing; and as we returned home, Suzon said to us,—

"There will be a storm before the day is over."

Her prediction pleased me; a storm was a happy
break in my monotonous life; and notwithstanding
my cowardice, I loved the thunder and lightning,
although they made me tremble in every limb when
the peals came too close together.

During the early part of the afternoon I wandered,
like a soul in pain, in the garden and the little wood.
I was bored to death, and said to myself dismally that
no adventure would ever happen to me, and that I was
fated to live always with my aunt.

Toward four o'clock, returning to the house, I went
up to the second-story hall; and, with my face glued
to the pane of a large window, I amused myself
by watching the clouds which piled themselves up
over Buisson, and brought us the storm predicted
by Suzon.

I asked myself whence they came, what they had
seen on their way, what they could tell me,— me who
knew nothing of life and of the world, and who longed
to see and to know. They were formed behind that
horizon which I had never passed, and which hid from
me mysteries, splendours,— at least, I hoped so, —
joys, and pleasures on which I meditated inwardly.

I was diverted from my reflections by noticing that
Perrine, hidden away in a snug corner, was being em-

braced by a big rustic, who had put his arm around her waist.

I opened the window quickly, and cried, clapping my hands,—

"Very good, Perrine; I see you, Mademoiselle!"

Perrine, in a fright, seized her sabots and fled for refuge to the stable. The big rustic pulled off his hat, and looked at me with a silly smile that stretched his mouth from ear to ear.

I was laughing with all my might, when a light carriage, which I had not heard approach, entered the courtyard. A man leaped to the ground, said some words to the servant who was with him, and looked about to find some one to speak to.

But Perrine, whose white cap I saw peeping over the barred window of the stable, did not budge, and her lover had thrown himself flat on his stomach behind a heap of straw. As to myself, stupefied before this apparition, I had drawn one of the blinds of the window, and was watching without making a movement.

The unknown cleared in two strides the dilapidated flight of steps, and looked for a bell that never existed; seeing which, and patience not being his dominant quality, he rapped loudly with his fist upon the door.

My aunt and Suzon rushed together to open it, and I certify that from that moment I had the most favourable opinion of his courage, for he did not show the slightest fear. He bowed lightly, and I made out from his gestures that the threatening skies having alarmed him, he was asking shelter at Buisson.

In fact, the storm broke with great violence at that very moment; there was just time to put the horse and carriage under shelter.

Solitude is said to create timidity, but in certain cases it produces just the contrary effect. Having come in contact with no one, and having no one to compare myself with, I had the greatest self-confidence, and I was absolutely ignorant of that strange feeling which annihilates the most brilliant faculties, and makes the most clever men stupid.

Nevertheless, in the face of this adventure, which seemed as if evoked by my thoughts, my heart beat wildly, and I hesitated so long to enter the salon that I was still at the door when the curé arrived, all dripping, but in great good-humour.

"Monsieur le Curé," I cried, rushing toward him, "there is a man in the salon!"

"Very well, Reine; a farmer, no doubt?"

"Not at all, Monsieur le Curé; it is a real man!"

"How a real man?"

"I mean to say that it is neither a curé nor a peasant, but a young man, well dressed. Let us go in, quick."

We entered, and I almost uttered a cry of surprise

when I noticed that my aunt wore a really gracious
expression, and that she was smiling agreeably at the
unknown, who, seated opposite her, seemed as much
at his ease as if he were at home.

For that matter, his appearance alone would have
been enough to brighten the gloomiest disposition.
He was tall, of good weight, with a face cheerful,
fresh, and open. His blond hair was cut short, he
had a mustache pointed at the ends, a well-shaped
mouth, and white teeth, which a frank and natural
laugh let one often see. All his person breathed
lightheartedness and the joy of living.

He rose on seeing us enter, and waited a moment
for my aunt to present him. But that ceremony
was as little known to her as to the inhabitants
of Greenland, and he presented himself as Paul
de Conprat.

"De Conprat!" cried the curé; "are you the son of
that excellent Commandant de Conprat whom I used
to know?"

"My father is commandant, it is true, Monsieur le
Curé. You have known him?"

"He did me a kindness many years ago! An admi-
rable, an excellent man!"

"I know that every one loves my father," answered
Monsieur de Conprat, his face brighter than ever.
"It is always a fresh pleasure to me to have evi-
dence of it."

"But," resumed the curé, "are you not a relative of Monsieur de Pavol?"

"Certainly, a third cousin."

"Here is his niece," said the curé, presenting me.

Notwithstanding my inexperience, I saw very clearly that Monsieur de Conprat's look expressed a certain admiration.

"I am enchanted to make the acquaintance of so charming a cousin," he said to me in a tone of conviction, holding out his hand.

The compliment gave me a pleasant little thrill, and I placed my hand in his without the least embarrassment.

"Not precisely cousins," said the curé, with a jubilant air; "Monsieur de Pavol is only Reine's uncle by marriage; his wife was a Mademoiselle de Lavalle."

"It makes no difference," cried Monsieur de Conprat; "I am not going to renounce our relationship. Besides, if you look carefully, you will find marriages between my family and that of de Lavalle."

We fell to talking like three good comrades, and it seemed to me as if we had always seen and known one another, and been friends. I had that curious feeling as if what was taking place before one's eyes had already happened at some distant time,— a time so distant that one preserved only a vague and half-effaced memory of it.

But when I ran over in my mind all the heroes of

romance that I knew, I could not find a single one as plump as my own.   He was stout,— there was not the shadow of doubt about that,— but so good, so light-hearted, so witty, that this physical defect became instantly in my eyes a transcendent virtue.   Soon even my imaginary heroes seemed totally shorn of charm.   Notwithstanding their figures, which were elegant and always slight, they were blotted out, totally blotted out, by this good, plump fellow, jolly and jocund, whom I mentally endowed with a host of accomplishments.

Meanwhile, although the storm had diminished in violence, the rain had not ceased; and the hour for dinner approaching, my aunt invited Paul de Conprat to share it with us.   He declared at once that he was as hungry as a cannibal, and accepted with an alacrity which charmed me.

I slipped out for an instant to face Suzon's bad temper.

"Suzon," I said, entering the kitchen excitedly, "Monsieur de Conprat is going to dine with us.   Have we a large fowl, milk, strawberries, and cherries?"

"*Hé! Seigneur!* here's a fuss!" grumbled Suzon. "There is what there is! there now!"

"Really and truly, Suzon! but answer me now.   A capon perhaps will not be enough."

"It is not a capon, Mademoiselle, it is a turkey; just take a look."

And Suzon quickly, with an air of pride, opened the oven and let me admire the bird, which, well fattened by her cares and those of Perrine, must have weighed at least twelve pounds. The browning skin puffed up here and there, showing the delicacy and tenderness of the meat which it covered, and offering to my delighted eyes a most joyful sight.

"Bravo!" I said. "But the curds, Suzon, are they a success? Is there a good deal of them? And the salad, look carefully to the dressing!"

"I am accustomed to succeed in what I undertake, Mademoiselle. Besides, this gentleman is neither a prince nor an emperor, I suppose. He is a man like any other, and will put up with what is given him."

"A man like any other, Suzon!" I said with indignation. "You have not seen him, then?"

"*Ma foi!* yes, Mademoiselle, I have seen and have heard him, I can truly say that. Is it allowable for a Christian man to beat with all his might on the door of an honest house as he did? After that, fall in love with him if you wish!"

I opened my mouth to answer sharply, but stopped short, prudently reflecting that, to show her resentment and provoke me, Suzon was quite capable of letting the turkey burn.

A few moments later we passed into the diningroom, and I could not refrain from casting a melancholy glance at the hangings, which, dirty and worn, fell in rags. To make matters worse, Suzon had a most singular fashion of laying the cloth. Three salt-cellars ranged themselves in the middle of the table after the fashion of an épergne. The silver was thrown helter-skelter; the bottles crowded one another; while the one and only carafe was placed so that each guest had to nearly dislocate himself to grasp it, the table being three times too large. For the first time in my life, I had an intuition that all the laws of symmetry were violated by Suzon's fantastic taste. But Monsieur de Conprat had one of those happy dispositions that look at everything on the bright side. And then he had the faculty of identifying himself with any place in which he found himself.

He looked at the table cheerfully, and swallowed his soup, talking without stopping, complimented Suzon, and uttered genuine expressions of delight at the sight of the turkey.

"It must be confessed, Monsieur le Curé," said he, "that life is a happy invention, and that Heraclitus was endowed with a strong dose of stupidity."

"Do not speak ill of philosophers," answered the curé; "they have their good points."

"You are too kind, Monsieur le Curé. For my part, if I were the government I would turn out the lunatics and put the philosophers in their place, taking care not to separate them, so that they might be able the better to destroy one another."

"What is it, this Heraclitus?" said my aunt.

"An idiot, Madame, who spent his time in whining. It was ridiculous, *mon Dieu!* and to have succeeded in imposing himself on posterity!"

"Perhaps," insinuated I, "he had lived with many aunts, and that had soured his disposition."

Monsieur de Conprat looked at me in astonishment, and broke into a loud laugh. The curé stared; but my aunt, busy with the turkey which she was carving skilfully, I must admit, had not heard.

"History is silent on this point, my cousin."

"In any case," I resumed, "beware of attacking the men of antiquity; Monsieur le Curé will tear out your eyes."

"Ah, the villains! how they plagued me! I have kept only one souvenir of them,—that of the impositions they caused me!"

"Permit me," said the curé, making an effort to bring his friends to the surface, and about to swamp himself completely in my opinion,—"permit me; you cannot deny certain noble virtues, certain heroic acts, which —"

"Delusions, delusions!" interrupted Paul de Conprat. "They were insupportable villains; and because they are dead they are clothed with incredible virtues to humiliate us poor fellows who are living, and who are worth more than they. *Dieu!* what an excellent turkey!"

And while talking without stopping, he ate with an animation and appetite without equal.

The slices heaped on his plate disappeared with a rapidity so remarkable that there was a moment when my aunt, the curé, and I remained, fork in air, watching him in silent astonishment.

"I gave you fair warning," he said, laughing, "that I was as hungry as a cannibal,— a hunger that comes to me, by the way, three hundred and sixty-five times a year."

"What a sum you must pay out for your table!" cried my aunt, whose peculiarity it was to seize on the commercial side of things, and to say what she ought not to say.

"Twenty-three thousand three hundred and seventy-seven francs, Madame," answered Monsieur de Conprat, in all seriousness.

"It is not possible," stammered my aunt, stupefied.

"You seem very happy, Monsieur," said the curé, rubbing his hands.

"Am I happy, Monsieur le Curé? I believe so, thoroughly. And look, frankly now, is it very natural to be unhappy?"

"Sometimes," answered the curé, smiling.

"Ah, bah! unhappy persons are generally so through their own fault, because they take life at cross purposes. You see, unhappiness does not exist; it is human stupidity which exists."

"But that is already an unhappy circumstance," said the curé.

"Sufficiently negative in itself, Monsieur le Curé; and because my neighbour is a fool, it does not follow that I should imitate him."

"You love a paradox, Monsieur?"

"Not at all; but I am provoked when I see so many people make their lives gloomy through an unhealthy imagination. I suppose they do not eat enough, that they live on larks or a boiled egg, and derange the brain at the same time as the stomach. I adore life; I think that every one should find it delightful, and that it has but one fault,— it must end, and that so quickly."

The turkey, the salad, the curds, all were devoured; and my aunt looked with a face which was no longer gracious at the skeleton of the bird on which she had planned to feast for several days. We were about to leave the table, when Suzon half opened the door, and poking her head through, said aggressively, —

"I have made some coffee; shall I bring it?"

"Who gave you permission — " began my aunt.

"Yes, yes," I said, interrupting quickly; "bring it at once."

I could have embraced her for this happy thought, but my aunt did not share my feelings. She disappeared in order to go and quarrel with Suzon, and we did not see her again, except in the salon.

"You have an excellent cook, Cousin," said Paul de Conprat, sipping his coffee.

"Yes, but such a scold!"

"That is a detail simply."

"And my aunt, what do you think of her?" I asked in a confidential tone.

"Well — rather majestic," answered Monsieur de Conprat, a little embarrassed.

"Ah, majestic! you would like to say disagreeable?"

"Reine!" murmured the curé.

"Oh, well, let us talk of something else, Monsieur le Curé; but I should really like to have my cousin's happy disposition, and find the good side of my aunt."

"Have a little practical philosophy, charming cousin; it supplies a solid basis for happiness, and is the only philosophy which seems to me to have any common-sense."

"What a pity that you could not have been my aunt; how we should have loved each other!"

"I can answer for that," he cried, laughing; "and we should have no need of philosophy to arrive at that result. But if it is the same to you, I would prefer not to change my sex, and to be your uncle."

"I should ask nothing better, because I am not like Francis I.; for my part, I have a pronounced antipathy to women."

"Truly," he replied, laughing with all his might, "you know the tastes of Francis I.?"

The curé made a gesture of despair, to which Monsieur de Conprat returned an expressive wink which seemed to say, "Don't be disturbed; I understand."

This pantomime irritated me, and I made a desperate attempt to grasp its hidden meaning.

"Speaking of uncles," I said, "you know Monsieur de Pavol very well?"

"Yes, very; my estate is within a league of his."

"And his daughter, what is she like?"

"I played with her often when she was a child, but for four years I have lost sight of her. She is said to be very beautiful."

"How much I should like to be at Pavol!" I sighed; "we should see each other often."

"Who knows, little cousin?—perhaps I should no longer please you if you knew me better. Nevertheless, I can truly say that I am a good fellow; and except that I have a passion for turkey, and love pretty women to the point of folly, I do not know that I have any small vices."

"To love pretty women is certainly no fault. For my part, I detest ugly people,—my aunt, for example. But to compare a turkey to a pretty woman is scarcely flattering to the latter, Cousin."

"It is true; I admit that my choice of words was unhappy."

"I pardon you," I said vivaciously. "Now, do you think me pretty?"

For two hours at least, I had been saying over and over in my inmost soul that I must not let the opportunity escape of enlightening myself by a frank and competent opinion on a subject of thrilling interest to me. Since the beginning of dinner I had waited impatiently for the time to ask my question. Not that I had any doubts as to the answer; but to hear absolutely directly, and face to face, that one is pretty, from some one other than a curé, is truly delicious.

"Pretty, my cousin! you are simply lovely! I have never seen more beautiful eyes nor a prettier mouth."

"How delightful! and how agreeable men are, whatever my aunt may say!"

"Does not your aunt like men? She has passed the age of coquetry, it is true."

"Coquetry! I have never heard of it. Do you think one should be a coquette?"

"Without doubt, Cousin; in my eyes, it is a great accomplishment."

"You have never told me this, Monsieur le Curé," I cried.

During this conversation the unhappy curé had a foretaste of the pains of purgatory. He mopped his face, and had great difficulty in swallowing his coffee, which seemed to him very bitter.

"Monsieur de Conprat is laughing at you," he said to me.

"Are you really, Cousin?"

"Not at all," answered Paul de Conprat, who had the appearance of being highly amused. "To my mind, a woman who is not a coquette is not a woman."

"Very good; I will try to become one, then."

"Let us go into the salon, Mademoiselle de Lavalle," said the curé, rising.

"Ah," thought I, "now the curé is provoked; yet I have said nothing amiss."

The rain had stopped, the clouds dispersed; and I proposed to Paul de Conprat to take a walk in the garden. Off we went, without waiting permission, followed by the curé, whose face was almost gloomy, and who thought that his ewe lamb was on the road to perdition.

We ran like two children through the wet grass; we soaked our feet and ankles, shouting with laughter. We talked, we chattered, I especially telling the events of my life, my little disappointments, my aspirations and antipathies.

Oh, that delightful, charming, delicious evening!

Monsieur de Conprat climbed into a cherry-tree, and shaking it violently, let fall on me all the rain-drops that it held. With his mouth full of cherries, he cried out from the top of the tree that the rain-drops shone in my beautiful hair like an ideal crown, and that he had never seen anything so beautiful.

"And Suzon," I said to myself, "pretended that he was a man like any other. Is it possible one can be such a fool?"

We returned to the salon, where a great fire was made for us to dry ourselves. Seated side by side, Paul de Conprat and I, we talked on together in a subdued tone.

My aunt, stunned by my audacity, my freedom from restraint, and the delight which shone on my face, said not a word. The curé, charmed at my happiness, was nevertheless not so actively preoccupied as to forget to make a third with us. Oh, what a delightful evening!

At last Monsieur de Conprat rose to go, and we accompanied him into the courtyard.

He said good-by warmly to the curé, and thanked my aunt; then, coming to me, he took my hand and said in a low tone,—

"I should have liked this evening never to end, Cousin."

"And I too! but you will come again, will you not?"

"Certainly, and very soon, I hope."

He lifted my hand to his lips; and it must truly be the case that human nature has, at the bottom, a great depth of perversity, for this homage gave me a pleasure so new, keen, and perfect that I had the indecorous idea — *mon Dieu!* must I confess it?— yes, I had the idea, which I did not put into execution, of throwing myself on his neck and embracing him on both cheeks, notwithstanding my aunt, and notwithstanding the curé, who watched us like some new kind of dragon,— an excellent dragon, chubby and genial.

CHAPTER VII.

MY mind was for some days after the departure of
Monsieur de Conprat in a beatific state which
it would be difficult for me to describe. I had mani-
fold sensations which showed themselves outwardly
in gambols and pirouettes, for this latter exercise
had for a long time been my fashion of expressing a
multitude of feelings.

After pirouetting wildly, I would throw myself on
the grass, and looking at the sky would day-dream
over many things, while really not thinking at all.
That delightful mental state, when the mind is in a
kind of drowsiness, a dreamy tranquillity which re-
sembles sleep, although it may be very wakeful, has
furnished me the sweetest food for recollection.

From this time, too, dates my passionate love for the sky, which since then has always seemed to sympathize with my thoughts, were they depressed or cheerful, serious or trifling.

When I had allowed my imagination to lose itself in shady byways, so obscure that it had to grope its way, I would bring it back to the light and let it survey Monsieur de Conprat. I laughed at the remembrance of his frank face, his pleasant smile, and his white teeth. I loved the kiss he gave my hand, and I experienced a veritable glee in thinking that, had I carried out my idea, I should have kissed him on both cheeks. I experienced these delightful sensations a long while, until a time came when I began to ask myself why my mind passed through these divers phases.

But when I reached this delicate question I was all in the dark, and my imagination had to deal with such vaporous fancies that, in despair of the task, I abandoned the attempt, in order to think again of a mouth which pleased me, of eyes which had smiled at me, and of an expression which I had firmly decided never to forget.

But those fantastic personages, my thoughts, did not leave me long in peace, and little by little, I fell into their power. Thus I was all uncertainty, until one day, bethinking me to corroborate certain impressions by those of my chosen heroines, I was enlightened on a leading point.

I discovered that I was in love, and that love was the most delightful thing in the world. The discovery filled me with the keenest joy. In the first place, because my life was beautified by a charm which, though undefined, was none the less real; next, because if I loved I was certainly loved in return. I, in fact, loved Monsieur de Conprat because he had seemed to me charming, consequently the sight of me ought to produce the same ravages in his heart, because he thought me ravishing. My logic, coupled with complete inexperience, went no further, and was amply sufficient to confirm my reasoning and to make me happy.

One discovery led to another, and I came to think that charity could have played only a very insignificant rôle in the love which Francis I. felt for ladies in general, and Anne de Pisseleu in particular; that love was not in the least like affection, for I adored my curé, and had not the least desire to embrace him, while I should not have had to be invited to throw myself on Paul de Conprat's neck; that it was perfectly ridiculous to assume a mysterious and evasive tone in speaking of so natural a thing, in which evidently there was not the shadow of harm.

But a curé, I thought, must necessarily have erroneous and extraordinary views of love, because, as he is not permitted to marry, he cannot fall in love. All the same, Francis I. was married and — I do not understand anything of all this, and must get some light.

There was such a chaos in my thoughts that notwithstanding my scornful prejudices on the subject of the curé's knowledge, I resolved to enter on this delicate subject with him.

The poor curé saw clearly that I was greatly troubled in mind, but he had too much finesse and good sense to seem to attach importance to impressions which would have acquired undue importance had he sought my confidence. He tried to distract me by every means in his reach; and taking up the habit of coming to Buisson every day, he prolonged the lessons indefinitely.

We were seated at our window. My aunt, who had been ailing for some time, had retired to her room; my thoughts were away in the moon, and the curé was exerting himself to explain my problems to me.

"See, now, what you have done, Reine! you have worked with kilograms instead of working with grams. And here, being given $\frac{3}{5}$ multiplied by —"

"Monsieur le Curé," I said, "guess what is the most fascinating thing in the world!"

"What is it, then, Reine?"

"Love, Monsieur le Curé."

"What are you talking about, ma petite?" cried the curé, uneasily.

"Oh, of something that I know very well," I answered, nodding my head sagely; "I even ask myself why you have never said a word to me about it, since one sees it every day."

"This comes from reading romances, Mademoiselle; you take seriously what is only imagination."

"How wrong it is to say what you do not think, Monsieur le Curé! You know perfectly well that people fall in love in real life, and that it is perfectly charming."

"It is a subject that does not concern young girls, Reine; you ought not to speak of it."

"How can it not concern young girls, when it is they who love and are loved?"

"How unfortunate I am," cried the curé, "to have to deal with such a head!"

"Don't say anything bad about my head, my dear curé; as for me, I am very fond of it, especially since Monsieur de Conprat thought it so pretty."

"Monsieur de Conprat was amusing himself with you, Reine. Make up your mind that he took you for a little girl of no account."

"Not at all," replied I, offended, "for he kissed my hand. And do you know the idea that came to me at that moment?"

"Let us hear it," answered the curé, who was on thorns.

"Well, then, Monsieur le Curé, I was on the point of throwing myself on his neck."

"What folly! One does not throw one's self on any one's neck unless one knows them intimately."

"Oh, yes, but he — And yet, had he been a woman, the idea would never have occurred to me."

"Why not, Reine? You talk nonsense."

"Oh, because — "

A silence followed this profound reply, and I stealthily examined the curé, who moved uneasily in his seat and took snuff to conceal his embarrassment.

"My good curé," I said in an insinuating tone, "if you were very good-natured — "

"What then, Reine?"

"Well, I should like to ask you a few little questions about some subjects which are running through my head."

The curé settled himself in his chair, like a man who suddenly makes a grand resolve.

"Very well, Reine; I am listening. It is much better to speak openly of what is occupying your thoughts than to puzzle your brain and not come to the point."

"I am not puzzling at all, Monsieur le Curé, and I am not wandering from the point; only I have thought a great deal of love because — "

"Because?"

"Oh, nothing. But to begin, tell me why it is that if you should kiss my hand I should think it ridiculous and not agreeable, although I love you with all my heart, while it is exactly the contrary when Monsieur de Conprat is in question."

"What? what? What is it you say, Reine?"

"I say that I found it very delightful to have Monsieur de Conprat kiss my hand, while if you —"

"But, ma petite, your question is absurd, and the feeling of which you speak means nothing, and is not worth considering."

"Ah, that is not my opinion. I have thought a good deal, and this is what I have discovered: it is that if Monsieur de Conprat's action seemed delightful to me, it is because he is young, and might marry me, while you are old, and, as a curé, can never marry."

"Yes, yes," the curé answered mechanically.

"For one always loves one's husband dearly; is it not so?"

"No doubt! No doubt!"

"Now, Monsieur le Curé, tell me whether it is true that men can love many women."

"I know nothing about it," said the curé, becoming irritated.

"But you certainly ought to know. Then can a married man love another woman than his wife, as Francis I. loved Anne de Pisseleu when he was married?"

"Francis I. was a *mauvais sujet*," cried the exasperated curé; "and Buckingham, whom you admire so much, was another!"

"*Mon Dieu!*" I exclaimed, "every one has his pecu-
liarities, and I do not see why one should consider it
a crime to love several women. Queen Claude and
the Duchess of Buckingham were perhaps like my
aunt. Besides, I am coming to find out that the
feelings do not keep themselves under control, and
they can no more refuse to love than I —"

"What? Reine!"

"Nothing, Monsieur le Curé; but I am afraid that I
have a weakness for *mauvais sujets*, for I find Buckingham especially charming."

"Listen, ma petite; I have tried to make you understand some things since you read Walter Scott, and
you appear to have understood absolutely nothing."

"Listen to me, my dear curé; your explanations
are not very lucid, and there is so much that is not
clear to my mind. All this is very strange," I continued musingly. "At least, tell me, Monsieur le
Curé, why love arouses your indignation?"

"Reine," said the curé, out of patience, "this is
enough. You have such a way of putting your questions that it is impossible to answer you. I say to
you in all seriousness that there are subjects of
which you should not speak, and which you cannot
understand, because you are too young."

The curé put his hat under his arm and departed.
I ran to the doorstep and cried, —

"You may say what you will, my dear curé, but I

know perfectly well what love is; it is the most delightful thing in the world! *Vive l'amour!*"

The curé let two days go by without coming to Buisson; therefore, full of contrition at having been so teasing, on the third day I took my way to the *presbytère* to beg his pardon. I found him in his kitchen before a frugal breakfast, which he was eating with equal animation and appetite.

"Monsieur le Curé," I said in a fairly humble tone, "are you angry?"

"A little, petite Reine; you will never listen to me."

"I promise not to speak of love again, Monsieur le Curé."

"Try, above all, Reine, not to think of things which you do not understand."

"Oh, that I do not understand!" I cried, taking fire immediately; "I understand perfectly, and in spite of all the curés on the earth, I will maintain that —"

"Come," interrupted the discouraged curé; "here you are in fault already!"

"It is true, my dear curé; but I assure you that a curé understands nothing at all of these things."

"And Reine de Lavalle no more. I will go and give you your lesson to-day, ma petite."

And in this fashion ended the most serious dispute I ever had with my curé.

Nevertheless, as the days went by and Paul de Conprat did not return, my nervous system began to give
way and showed an irritability which boded ill. A
month after my memorable adventure, I had lost my
hopes and my tranquillity; and, my *ennui* contribut-
ing, I fell into a state of gloomy depression.

It was then that the curé quarrelled with my aunt,
who turned him out of the house.

Seated under the window of the salon, I heard the
following conversation: —

"Madame," said the curé, "I have come to speak
to you about Reine."

"Why about her?"

"The child is tired and ill, Madame. Monsieur
de Conprat's visit opened to her intelligence hori-
zons upon which light had already been thrown by
some romances she had read. She must have some
diversion."

"Diversion! Where would you like me to take her?
I am not able to move. I am ill!"

"For that reason I do not count on you to furnish
her diversion, Madame. Monsieur de Pavol must be
written to, and asked to take her to his house for
some time."

"Monsieur de Pavol written to! Certainly not!
The child would never want to come back."

"That is possible; but it is a secondary consideration, which we can take up later. Inasmuch as she

is destined to live some day or other in the world, it seems to me necessary that she should change her mode of life, and see many things of which she has no conception."

"I will not hear of it, Monsieur le Curé. Reine shall not leave here!"

"But, Madame," replied the curé, growing warm, "I say again that the matter does not admit of delay. Reine is depressed; her brain is active and constantly working. I am certain that she fancies herself in love with Monsieur de Conprat."

"It is all the same to me," said my aunt, who was entirely incapable of understanding the curé's reasons.

"It has been said that solitude is the Devil's advocate, Madame; and it is perfectly true with youth. Solitude is injurious to Reine; a little diversion will make her forget what is really only a childish impression."

"What ridiculous ideas the curé has!" I thought. "To treat lightly such a serious thing, and to believe that some day I shall forget Monsieur de Conprat!"

"Monsieur le Curé," said my aunt, in her dryest tone, "mind your own business. I will act according to my judgment and not yours."

"Madame, I love the child with all my heart, and will not hear of her being unhappy," answered the curé, in a tone I did not recognize. "You have buried her at Buisson; you have never given her the slightest gratification; and I can say that, had it not been for me, she would have grown up in ignorance and stupidity, and would have been a wild, half-nourished little plant. I repeat, Monsieur de Pavol must be written to."

"This is too much!" cried my aunt, furious. "Am I not the mistress in my own home? Leave the house, Monsieur le Curé, and don't put foot in it again."

"Very well, Madame; I know now what I must do, and I see clearly to-day that if I have not acted sooner, it is because I was blinded by the selfish pleasure of seeing my little Reine constantly."

The curé found me in the road all in tears.

"Is it possible, my good curé,—turned out of the house on my account? What is going to become of us if we cannot see each other any more?"

"You heard the discussion, my little child?"

"Yes, yes; I was under the window. Ah, what a woman! what —"

"Come, come; be calm, Reine," said the curé, who was all flushed and trembling. "This very night I shall write to your uncle."

"Write soon, my dear curé; perhaps he will come for me at once."

"Let us hope so," said the curé, with a smile kindly but a little sad.

But other duties prevented his writing that same
night to Monsieur de Pavol; and the next day my
aunt, who had been struggling for some weeks against
disease, fell dangerously ill. Five days later death
knocked at the door of Buisson, and changed the
aspect of my life.

CHAPTER VIII.

I TOOK refuge at the *presbytère* immediately after
the death of my aunt, who never once asked to
see me during her illness, and who was nursed de-
votedly by Suzon.

The curé had written to Monsieur de Pavol to inform
him that Madame de Lavalle was ill; but the progress
of the disease was so rapid that my uncle received the
despatch announcing its fatal result before he had
been able to answer the curé's letter. He telegraphed
at once that it would be impossible for him to be present at the funeral service.

The next day we received a letter in which he said
that as he had not yet recovered from an attack of
gout, he should not come to Buisson. He begged the

curé to take me, a few days later, to C——, when he hoped to be well enough to come there to meet me.

My aunt was buried without pomp and without ceremony. She had not been loved, and departed for the other world without a long train of mourners.

I returned from the interment, making many efforts to feel a little sorry, but could not. Whatever may have been the reproaches of my conscience, a feeling of deliverance was predominant in my head and my heart. Nevertheless, had I known the saying of a celebrated man, I should certainly have appropriated it, and I declare that I should have cried in a superb outburst of misanthropy, —

"I know not what goes on in the heart of a wretch; but I know that of an honest little girl, and what I see there frightens me."

But the saying being entirely unknown to me, I could not use it to appease the manes of my aunt.

My uncle had fixed on the 10th of August as the day for me to leave; it was now the 8th, and I was passing the two days with the curé, whose cheerfulness departed hourly at the thought of our separation.

Tuesday morning he prepared for me an excellent breakfast, and we took our places face to face for the last time, to try to force ourselves to eat. But each mouthful choked me; and I had all the trouble in the world to keep back my tears.

The poor curé had passed the night without sleep.

He was too full of grief for that; and, besides, not being able to accompany me to C——, he had writ-ten my uncle a letter of seventeen pages, as I learned later on, in which he enumerated my accomplish-ments, great and small and medium. As to faults, they were not mentioned.

"My dear little child," he said to me after a long silence, "you will never forget your old curé?"

"Never! Never!" I said earnestly.

"And you will not forget my counsels either. Dis-trust your imagination, petite Reine. I may compare it to a beautiful flame which lightens and vivifies the mind when judiciously fed, but which, if given too much nourishment, becomes a bonfire which spreads to the house, and the conflagration leaves behind it only ashes and dross."

"I will strive to manage the flame wisely, Mon-sieur le Curé; but I confess that I am very fond of bonfires."

"Yes; but beware of a conflagration! Don't let us play with fire, Reine."

"Just a little bonfire, Monsieur le Curé,— that is charming. And if one is afraid of a conflagration, one can throw cold water on the grate."

"But where is the cold water to be found, ma petite?"

"Ah, I do not know yet, but some day perhaps I shall find out."

"God grant you may not, my dear little child! Cold water means disillusion and heartaches; and I shall pray fervently every day that they may be removed from your path."

Tears came to my eyes when I heard my curé speak in this way, and I swallowed a great glass of water to keep down my emotion.

"Before I leave you," I resumed, "I ought to tell you that I believe I have a very strong taste for coquetry."

"It is the weak spot with all women, that I know," said the curé, with his kindly smile, "but not a great fault, Reine. As to the rest, mixing with the world will teach you to govern your feelings, and, besides, your uncle will be able to advise you."

"How charming the world will be, Monsieur le Curé! and I am sure to please, being so pretty —"

"Without doubt, without doubt; but distrust exaggerated compliments, and be on your guard against vanity."

"Bah! it is so natural to love to please; there is no harm in that."

"Hum! That is a rather lax doctrine," answered the curé, ruffling up his hair. "Eh, well, your arguments are those of your age, and, Heaven be thanked, you have not yet to say, as in Ecclesiastes, all is vanity, and nothing but vanity."

"What an exaggerator that Ecclesiastes is! and

then he is so old. I fancy that his ideas must be superannuated."

"Come, come; let us leave the subject! I am perfectly aware that the Holy Scriptures and the thoughts of a poor country curé cannot be understood by a pretty young girl, who appears to me to have a very good opinion of her appearance."

He looked at me smiling, but his lips trembled, for the time for departure was close at hand.

"Be careful not to be cold on the way, Reine."

"But, Monsieur le Curé, it is the middle of August. It is stifling."

"It is true," answered the curé, who seemed a little dazed. "Then do not wrap too warmly, for fear of taking a chill."

We rose from the table, after vain attempts to nibble some bits of bread and pâté.

"I am so unhappy!" I cried, bursting suddenly into sobs. "I am so unhappy at leaving you, my dear curé!"

"Do not cry, do not cry! it is perfectly absurd," said the curé, not noticing that big tears were running down his own cheeks.

"Ah, my curé," I said, seized with sudden remorse, "I have been such a plague."

"No, no; you have been the joy of my life, my only happiness."

"What will become of you without me, my poor curé?"

The curé made no reply. He took some steps up and down the room, blowing his nose loudly, and succeeded in conquering the emotion which was choking him, and almost causing him to break into sobs.

The *maringote* was at the door. Perrine, in all her finery, was to go with me as far as C—— and put me in my uncle's arms. The farmer had been directed to drive us, in place of Suzon, who, thoroughly to her regret, remained provisionally in charge at Buisson. I told Jean to drive on; and the curé and I walked a little way so as to be longer together.

"I will write you every day, Monsieur le Curé."

"I do not ask so much as that, my dear child; write me once a month, and then very intimately."

"I will write you everything, absolutely everything, even my views on love."

"We shall see about that," said the curé, with an incredulous smile. "The life which you will lead will be so new to you, so full of amusements, that I do not count very much on your keeping your promise exactly."

Jean had stopped to wait for us, and I saw that we must part. I grasped my curé's hands, crying bitterly.

"Life has some very wretched moments, Monsieur le Curé!"

"They will pass, they will pass," he answered in a broken voice. "Good-by, my dear, good little child, do not forget me, and mistrust — mistrust —"

But he could not finish the sentence, and helped me hurriedly climb into the cart.

I took my aunt's old place, crushed on one side by a trunk which had lost its lock, and on the other by innumerable packages of the most outlandish shape, made up by Perrine.

"Good-by, my curé; good-by, my old curé," I cried.

He waved me an affectionate adieu, and turned back brusquely. Through my tears, I saw him stride away and put his hat on his head, — a proof absolute that his mind was not only in the most violent agitation, but really topsy-turvy.

After having sobbed for ten good minutes, I concluded that it was time to follow the advice of Perrine, which she kept repeating over and over, —

"You must be reasonable, Mamselle; you must be reasonable."

I thrust my handkerchief into my pocket, and set myself to thinking.

Truly, life is a very strange thing. Who would have believed, a fortnight before, that my dreams would have come true so promptly and that I should soon see Monsieur de Conprat? This cheerful idea chased the last clouds which darkened my spirits; and I began to note that the sky was blue, life sweet, and that aunts who go to heaven or purgatory are gifted with superior intelligence.

My second thought was of my uncle. I was much concerned as to the impression I should make on him; and I was sure that the black dress and the curious hat, which Suzon had stuck together, were perfectly ridiculous. The unhappy hat caused me a veritable torture,— I mean a mental torture. Made with *crêpe* which dated from the death of Monsieur de Lavalle, it had the look of a pancake which had been a play-ground for impertinent snails. It was evidently un-becoming; and this idea being unbearable, I took off my hat, I rolled it into a wad, and I put it in my pocket, the size and depth of which did honour to Suzon's practical genius.

Next, I was tormented by the fear of appearing stupid, for I knew that a multitude of things which seemed natural to all the world would be a source of surprise and wonder to me. I resolved, then, so as not to expose my self-esteem to the danger of ridi-cule, to hide my astonishments carefully.

These various preoccupations prevented me from finding the journey long; and I thought we were still far from C—— when we were just about reaching it. We went directly to the railway station after having passed through the town as rapidly as the stiff joints of our horse would permit.

My uncle being neither stout nor thin, I had natu-rally pictured him as both. I was therefore much astonished when I saw a genial gentleman, with a careless gait, approach the cart and cry,— if my uncle could ever cry,—

"Good-morning, my niece; I had really begun to think that I had made a mistake in expecting you."

He gave me his hand to help me down, and embraced me cordially.   After which, examining me from head to foot, he said to me,—

"Not taller than a fairy, but devilish pretty!"

"That is exactly my opinion, Uncle," I answered, dropping my eyes modestly.

"Ah, that is your opinion?"

"Yes, and that of my curé, and that of —   But here is a letter from the curé for you, Uncle."

"Why is he not here?"

"He was prevented by clerical duties."

"So much the worse; I should have been happy to see him.   You have no hat, Niece?"

"Yes, Uncle, it is in my pocket."

"In your pocket!   Why there?"

"Because it is hideous, Uncle."

"An excellent reason!   Who ever saw a hat carried in a pocket!   One cannot travel without a hat, ma petite.   Hurry and put it on, while I check your baggage."

Somewhat disconcerted by this reprimand, I replaced my hat on my head, not without proof that a journey in the pocket is not healthful for this product of human industry.

After this I said good-by to Jean and Perrine.

"Ah, Mamselle," said Perrine to me, "if you were a good and beautiful cow, I could not feel worse in leaving you."

"Many thanks," I said, half laughing, half crying. "Let us embrace and say good-by."

I kissed Perrine's firm red cheeks, on which, I greatly fear, more than one soft-spoken scamp had left kisses sly or resounding.

"Good-by, Jean."

"Good-by, Mamselle," said Jean, laughing stupidly, which was his way of showing his feelings.

A few moments after, I was in the train seated opposite my uncle, really scared and dizzy at the bustle of the station and the novelty of my position.

When I had recovered myself a little, I examined Monsieur de Pavol.

My uncle, of average height, well built, with broad shoulders and thick red hands not very well cared for, did not at first glance present an aristocratic appearance. He had a red face, high forehead, large nose, and hair like a brush cut very short; his eyes were small and piercing, and deep-sunk beneath eyebrows bushy and prominent. But under this commonplace exterior could be seen at once the man of the world and the man of family. His strongest feature, the one most striking, was his mouth. Clear-cut, strong, and fairly handsome, although the lower lip was a little thick, his mouth had an expression fine, ironical, humorous, crafty, and satirical which disconcerted the least timid and floored them on the spot. In observing it, one forgot entirely the commonplace in my uncle's face, or rather one found nothing commonplace in it, and had to admit that his rough features were a frame which brought out admirably his intellectual mouth.

My uncle did not talk much, and always slowly, but what he said was generally to the point. He sometimes used strong expressions, which produced a curious effect, because they were uttered slowly and quietly. He was only sixty years old; but being subject to frequent attacks of the gout, his mind was a little dulled by physical suffering. But if he had lost his old quickness of repartee, his mouth, by a movement nearly imperceptible, expressed all the shades of difference between irony, shrewdness, open ridicule, or satire; and I have seen persons annihilated before my uncle had uttered a word.

I was naturally too inexperienced to make at once a searching study of Monsieur de Pavol; but I watched him with the greatest interest. He, on his part, while reading the letter which I had brought him, threw at me, from time to time, a scrutinizing glance, as if to satisfy himself that my face did not contradict the curé's assertions.

"You look at me very fixedly, my niece," he said to me. "Do you think me handsome, perchance?"

"Not the least in the world!"

My uncle made a slight grimace.

"That is frankness, or I do not know it. And can you tell me why you are so pale?"

"Because I am dying of fear, Uncle."

"Fear! and of what?"

"We are going so fast,—it is frightful!"

"Ah, very good, I understand. It is your first journey. But do not be alarmed; there is no danger."

"And my cousin, Uncle, is she at Pavol?"

"Certainly; she will be greatly pleased to make your acquaintance."

My uncle asked me some questions about my aunt and my life at Buisson; then he took a newspaper and said not a word until we were at V——.

We there got into a landau, with two horses, which was to take us to Pavol. My heavy packages were piled in this elegant carriage as they best could be, and presented a sorry appearance which mortified me greatly.

Hardly were we in our seats than my uncle gave me a package of cakes to cheer me up, and plunged into a fresh newspaper.

This method of procedure began to irritate me.

Besides its being my way not to be long silent, I had a great many questions to ask; so when I had

grown used to the novelty of finding myself borne
along in a handsome, easy, well-upholstered carriage,
I ventured to break the silence.

"Uncle," I said, "if you don't care to read any
more, we might talk a little."

"Willingly, my niece," said my uncle, folding up
his paper at once. "I thought I was pleasing you
by leaving you to your thoughts. What are we going
to talk about? Shall it be the Eastern question, political economy, doll's dresses, or the habits of monkeys?"

"All these are of little interest to me; and as to
the habits of monkeys, I fancy, Uncle, that I know as
much on that subject as you."

"It is very possible," replied Monsieur de Pavol,
much astonished at my self-possession.

"Tell me, Uncle, are you not a little of a scamp?"

"Heh! what the devil do you say, my niece?"

"I ask you, Uncle, if you are not a little of a scamp
and a bully?"

"—— you, are you laughing at me?" cried my
uncle, using a word entirely unparliamentary.

"Don't be angry, Uncle; I am beginning a study of
morals, more interesting than the study of monkeys.
I want to know whether my aunt was right; she asserted that all men were scamps."

"Then your aunt had not common-sense."

"She had a great deal when she departed for the
other world, but not at any other time."

Monsieur de Pavol looked at me with evident astonishment.

"Ah, indeed, my niece! you have a rather crude way of expressing your thought! You did not get on, then, with Madame de Lavalle?"

"Not at all. She was very cross, and beat me more than once. Ask the curé, whom she turned out of the house on my account when he stood up for my rights. And how did it happen, Uncle, that you left me so long with her? She was a woman of the people, and you would not have liked her."

"When your parents died, Reine, my wife was very ill, and I was only too glad that my sister-in-law was willing to take charge of you. I saw you when you were six years old; you seemed then happy and well cared for, and since, upon my word, I had nearly forgotten you. I regret it now keenly, since you were not happy."

"You will keep me with you now always, Uncle?"

"Yes, certainly," said Monsieur de Pavol, with almost animation.

"When I say always, I mean until my marriage, for I shall marry soon."

"You will marry soon! What, you have hardly left the nursery, and you talk of marrying! Marriage is a foolish invention, understand that, my niece."

"Why?"

"Women are not worth a rap," said my uncle, in a tone of conviction.

I threw myself back into my corner, shocked, as I thought this estimate was not very flattering to my Aunt Pavol. When I had meditated over my uncle's remark, I answered, —

"But since I shall marry a man, it is all the same to me that women are not worth a rap. My husband will have to arrange matters with me as best he can."

"Here is logic for you! You know how to reason, it appears. Young girls are all crazy to marry, — it is a well-known fact."

"Does my cousin share my ideas?"

"Yes," replied my uncle, gloomily.

"Ah, so much the better," I said, rubbing my hands. "Is my cousin tall?"

"Tall and lovely," answered Monsieur de Pavol, complacently; "a veritable goddess and the delight of my eyes. But you will see her in a moment, for we are just arriving."

We were, in fact, turning into an avenue of huge elms which led to the château.

My cousin awaited us on the steps, and received me in her arms with the majesty of a queen according a favour to a subject.

"*Dieu!* how beautiful you are!" I exclaimed, looking at her with admiration.

It is certainly rare to meet absolutely beautiful women, but my cousin's beauty was so manifest as not to admit of a question. She was not always pleasing, her face being haughty and sometimes a little hard, but those who admired her least were obliged to say with my uncle,—

"She is devilish pretty!"

She had brown hair growing low on her forehead, a perfectly pure Grecian profile, a beautiful colour, dark eyelashes, and well-formed brows. Tall, strong, with a well-developed figure, she would have passed for more than eighteen had not her mouth, notwithstanding a little disdainful curve, which threatened to become too accentuated later, had signs of weakness, betraying early youth. Her step and her movements were slow and a little nonchalant, though always harmonious and without affectation. A friend of Monsieur de Pavol had said laughingly one day that at twenty-five she would resemble Juno line for line. The name clung to her.

I was suddenly seized with a veritable enthusiasm for my magnificent cousin; and my uncle was much amused at my astonishment.

"You have never seen beautiful women, then, my niece?"

"I have never seen anything at all, for I was buried alive in a hole."

"You should look in the glass, Reine; Monsieur de

Conprat told us the truth, that you were very pretty."

"Paul de Conprat?" I cried.

"It is a fact," said my uncle; "I had forgotten to speak to you of him. It seems that he took refuge at Buisson one stormy day?"

"I remember him well," I answered, blushing.

"Is he coming to breakfast on Monday, Blanche?"

"Yes, Father; the commandant has written a line to-day to accept the invitation. Who made your dresses, Reine?"

"Suzon,— a counterpart of my aunt in bad taste and stupidity," I answered viciously.

"We will make good the deficiency of your wardrobe to-morrow, my niece. Only have a little more respect for the memory of Madame de Lavalle. You did not love her; but she is dead, and peace to her soul. Come to dinner. Juno will show you your rooms afterward."

I passed a part of the night at my window in delicious dreams, and in watching the sombre masses of the great trees about Pavol, where I was to laugh, to weep, to amuse myself, to mourn, and to see my destiny accomplished.

I was so happy that night that my curé was hardly an appreciable unit in my recollections.

CHAPTER IX.

B^{UT} I beg that no one will believe me trifling and inconstant, for this forgetfulness was only momentary; and three days after my arrival at Pavol, I wrote my curé the following letter: —

MY DEAR CURÉ, — I have so many things to say, so many discoveries to tell you of, so many confidences to make, that I do not know where to begin. Picture to yourself that the sun is brighter here than at Buisson; that the trees are finer; that the flowers are fresher; that everything is delightful; that an uncle is one of Nature's happy inventions; and that my cousin is beautiful as a fairy. Though you should lecture me, scold me, and remonstrate well with me, my dear curé, you could not change my opinion that if Francis I. loved women as beautiful as Blanche de Pavol he had a singularly sound judgment. You yourself, Monsieur le Curé, even you, would fall in love with her at sight. But I confess that her queenly manner intimidates me a little, — me, whom nothing intimidates. And

then she is so tall; and I could have wished that she were
small, it would have consoled me a little, although I know
now that my figure, even if small, is lithe, elegant, and perfectly proportioned. All the same, a few inches more in
height, what difference could it have made, I ask you, to the
bon Dieu? Confess, Monsieur le Curé, that the *bon Dieu* is
sometimes very contrary.

I will not speak of my uncle, for I know that you know
him; but I see already that I shall love him, and that I have
made a conquest of him. It is a great pleasure to have a
good figure, my dear curé, very much greater than you would
like to admit; every one admires it, and when I am a grand-
mother, I will tell my grandchildren that it was the first and
most delightful discovery which I made when I went into the
world. But there is plenty of time to think of that.

Although I go from surprise to surprise, I am already perfectly accustomed to Pavol and the luxury which surrounds
me. Nevertheless, I should sometimes utter exclamations of
astonishment if I were not afraid of appearing ridiculous; I
conceal my impressions, but to you, my dear curé, I can confess that I am often greatly amazed.

We went to V—— day before yesterday to buy me an
outfit, Suzon's productions being decided horrors. Don't de-
lude yourself, my poor curé; notwithstanding your admiration
for certain gowns, I came here dressed like a fright, a perfect
fright.

Ah, what a pleasant thing a town is! I was delighted,
was wonder-struck, at the streets, the shops, the houses, the
churches; and Blanche was much amused at me, for she calls
V—— a hole on a hill. What would one call Buisson, then?
After a three hours' interview with the dressmaker and milli-

ner, my cousin, who is very devout, went to confession, and left me to make some purchases with the maid. My uncle had given me some money to purchase what was useful and practical; but do you believe that I cannot decide what is useful and practical? I began by going to a cake-shop, and stuffing myself with little cakes; I humbly acknowledge, my dear curé, that I have a passion for little cakes. While I gave myself up to this occupation, as necessary as agreeable, you will admit, — for after all it is an important duty to nourish this body of clay, — I noticed many very pretty things in a shop facing that of the confectioner. I went at once and bought forty-two little terra-cotta men, — all they had in the place. After that I not only had no money left, but I was deeply in debt, though that troubled me little, for I am rich. My cousin laughed a great deal, but my uncle scolded me. He wished me to understand that common-sense ought to guide every one, great or small, that it is useful at every age, and that without it one does foolish things; for example, one buys forty-two little terra-cotta men instead of supplying one's self with stockings and chemises. I heard this discourse with a contrite and humble air, my dear curé; but at its end, which was, on my word, very fine, my rebellious fancy pictured common-sense as having an ill-favoured body, a long, almost Roman nose, a face withered and sharp, and this individual resembled my aunt so much that, on the spot, I took a dislike to common-sense. Such was the result of my uncle's eloquence. Meantime I have forty-two little men weeping, smiling, grimacing, scattered about my room, and I am happy.

Last night I talked with Blanche about love, Monsieur le Curé. Why did you say to me that it was found only in books, and that it did not concern young girls? Ah, my curé,

9

my curé! I am afraid that you very often deceived me. We shall go into society when the first weeks of mourning have passed. My uncle thinks me very young, but I cannot stay at Pavol alone. If it were in question, you understand, Monsieur le Curé, that there would be only one thing to do, either to throw myself out of the window, or to set the house on fire.

It appears that I have good reason to expect a great success, because I am both pretty and the owner of a big *dot.* Blanche has informed me that a pretty face without a *dot* has little value, but that the two things combined make a perfect whole and a rare morsel. I am, then, my dear curé, a savoury mouthful, delicate and succulent, which will be envied, sought after, and swallowed in the twinkling of an eye, if I am willing to permit it. I shall not permit it, rest easy, at least until — But, *chut!*

And now, Monsieur le Curé, I am awaiting Monday with impatience, only I will not tell you why. On that day an event is to take place which makes my heart beat, — an event which makes me want to pirouette until I am out of breath, to throw my hat in the air, to dance, and to commit some folly. *Dieu!* what a beautiful thing life is!

But nothing is perfect, because you are not here, and I miss you very much. I cannot tell you how much, my poor curé. I should so love to make you admire the château and the well-kept gardens, so little like those at Buisson. I should so love to have you enjoy the generous and comfortable life which is led here. The smallest thing is arranged down to its minutest detail; and I really believe myself in a terrestrial paradise. Every moment I have some new cause for pleasure and admiration, and every moment I wish to share it with you. I

want you, I call you; but the echoes of this beautiful park are
silent.

Farewell, my dear, good curé; I do not embrace you, because one does not embrace a curé (I wonder why, for instance), but I send you all my heart holds for you, and it is
full of affection.   I adore you, Monsieur le Curé.

REINE.

It is a fact that I accustomed myself at once to
the atmosphere of luxury and elegance into which I
had been suddenly transplanted.   It is equally certain
that although Blanche was very friendly with me, and
had decided that we should be on intimate terms,
she overawed me during the first days that followed my
arrival at Pavol.   Her goddess-like carriage, her slight
air of haughtiness, and the idea that she had had much
more experience than I,—all this overpowered me and
prevented my being very unreserved with her.   But
that impression lasted only as long as an icicle under
an April sun; and after a conversation which we had
Sunday morning in my room, the prestige with which
I had endowed her disappeared entirely.

I was still in bed, half asleep and coddling myself
deliciously, opening an eye from time to time to
survey with delight my bright and comfortable room,
my little terra-cotta men, and the trees which I could
see through the open window.   Blanche came in, in
a long wrapper, her hair on her shoulders, and an
anxious look on her face.

"As beautiful as the most beautiful of Walter Scott's heroines," I said, watching her with admiration.

"Petite Reine," she said, seating herself on the foot of my bed, "I have come to talk with you."

"So much the better.   But I am not entirely awake, and my ideas are befogged."

"Even if it is about marriage?" asked Blanche, who knew already my opinion on this important subject.

"Marriage! I am very wide awake!" I said, raising myself up suddenly.

"Do you want to be married, Reine?"

"Do I want to be married! What a question! I do indeed, and as soon as possible. I adore men; I love them much more than women, except when the women are as beautiful as you."

"One should not say that one adores men," said Blanche, severely.

"Why not?"

"I do not know exactly why; but I assure you that it is not proper for a young girl."

"So much the worse. Besides, I think it is!" I answered, snuggling down under the covers.

"Child!" exclaimed Blanche, looking at me with a sort of pity which was rather offensive. "I have come to talk to you about my father, Reine."

"What about him?"

"Listen.   I am like you in wanting to marry some

day or other; my father has already refused many good offers, but that is all the same to me, because I am in no hurry. I am willing to wait until I am twenty; but I should like to know if he is going to object always to my marriage."

"You must ask him."

"Ah, that is the difficulty," answered Blanche, a little embarrassed. "I confess that I am afraid of my father, or rather that he overawes me."

Filled with surprise, I raised myself on my elbow, and pushed back the hair which fell over my face to see my cousin better. In that moment she fell from the clouds of Olympus, on which I had placed her; and under the beautiful figure of Juno, I discovered a young girl, who no longer intimidated me.

"No one overawes me," I cried, seizing my pillow and sending it flying into the middle of the room.

Blanche looked at me in astonishment.

"What are you doing, Reine?"

"Oh, it is a habit of mine. When I was at Buisson, I always threw my pillow, no matter where, to provoke Suzon, whom it always put in a passion."

"As Suzon is not here, I advise you to give up the habit. But to return to what we were saying, do you think you have the courage to have an argument with my father on the subject of marriage, which he is always abusing?"

"Yes, yes; I am very strong on arguing, you will

see. I will attack my uncle to-night, and will manage things easily."

During dinner I addressed an expressive pantomime to my cousin, to let her know that I was going to enter the lists. My uncle, who scented some danger, watched under his shaggy eyebrows; and. Blanche, already disconcerted, urged me by a sign to be quiet. But I snapped my fingers, coughed loudly, and leaped boldly into the arena.

"Uncle, can persons have children without being married?"

"No, certainly not!" answered my uncle, whom my question seemed to amuse greatly.

"Would it be a misfortune if humanity were to disappear?"

"Hum! That is a grave question. Philanthropists would say yes, and misanthropes, no."

"But your opinion, Uncle?"

"I have not given the matter consideration. Nevertheless, as Providence has done all things well, I vote for the perpetuation of the human race."

"Then, Uncle, you are not consistent when you abuse marriage."

"Ah, ha!" said my uncle.

"Since one cannot have children unless married, and you vote for the perpetuation of the human race, it follows that you ought to approve of marriage for every one."

" *Ventre Saint-Gris!* " exclaimed Monsieur de Pa-vol, working his lip with so satirical an air that Blanche became red; "this is what it is to argue. What is marriage, then, in your opinion, my niece?"

"Marriage, " I said enthusiastically, "is the most beautiful of all the institutions in the world,— a life-long union with him whom one loves! They sing and dance together; he kisses her hand. It is charming!"

"He kisses her hand! Why the hand, my niece?"

"Because it is — oh, that is an idea of mine," I said, addressing a smile full of mystery to my past.

"Marriage is an institution which delivers a victim to the executioner," growled my uncle.

"Ah!"

Juno and I protested with all our might.

"Who is the victim, Father?"

"The man, *parbleu!* "

"So much the worse for the men," I answered in a decided tone; "let them defend themselves. As for me, I am ready to transform myself into an executioner."

"What are you trying to get at now, young ladies?"

"At this, Uncle: Blanche and I are strong advo-cates of marriage, and we have resolved to put our theories into practice. I wish it to be as soon as possible."

"Reine!" cried my cousin, stunned at my audacity.

"I have spoken the truth, Blanche; only you are

willing to wait, while as for me, I have not the patience."

"Indeed, my niece! I suppose, however, that you are not in love?"

"Naturally," said Blanche, laughing; "she does not know a soul."

Since my arrival at Pavol I had often thought of my love and of Monsieur de Conprat; and I often asked myself if I ought not to tell my cousin this inmost secret of my heart. But all things considered, I decided in this case to break all my principles and to join the Arab in finding with him that silence is golden. Nevertheless, at this assertion by Blanche, and notwithstanding my fixed resolution to keep my secret, I was on the point of letting it out; but I managed to overcome the temptation to speak.

"In any case, I shall be in love some day or other, for one cannot live without loving."

"Indeed! Where have you got your ideas, Reine?"

"But, Uncle, that is life," I answered composedly. "Just consider Walter Scott's heroines a moment,— how they love and are loved."

"Ah, did the curé permit you to read romances and give you a course on love?"

"My poor curé! How I provoked him about that very thing! As to romances, Uncle, he did not wish me to have them; he even carried off the key of the

library, but I got in through the window by breaking a pane."

"Here is a promising child! As a consequence, you are in haste to day-dream and moon about love."

"I do not moon at all, Uncle, — above all, on that subject, for I know perfectly well what I am talking about."

"*Diable!*" said my uncle, laughing, "and yet you say that you are not in love with any one."

"It is true," I answered quickly, confused enough at my blunder. "But do you not think, Uncle, that reflection can supply the lack of experience?"

"Most assuredly! I am convinced of it, especially on such a subject. And then you seem to me to have a very well-ordered mind."

"I am only logical, Uncle. Tell me, does one ever love any man but one's husband?"

"No, never!" answered Monsieur de Pavol, smiling.

"Very well; since one loves no man but one's husband, and one naturally always loves one's husband dearly, and one is not able to live without love, I conclude that it is necessary to marry."

"Yes; but not before twenty-one, young ladies."

"It is all the same to me," said Blanche.

"But it is not all the same to me; I can never wait five years!"

"You will have to wait five years, Reine; at least, unless in some extraordinary case."

"What do you call an extraordinary case, Uncle?"

"A match so suitable in every respect that it would be absurd to refuse it."

This modification of my uncle's programme was so delightful to me that I jumped up to pirouette.

"Then I am sure of my case," I cried, taking to my heels.

I took refuge in my room, where Juno soon appeared, with a majestic air.

"How brazen you are, Reine!"

"Brazen! Is that the way you thank me when I did what you wanted me to?"

"Yes; but you say things so point blank."

"It is my way; I like things on the square."

"Then it seemed as if you wanted to vex my father."

"I should be sorry indeed to vex him. He charms me with his satirical face, and I already love him dearly. But to keep to the subject, Blanche, it was he who provoked us, by declaiming against marriage, and, after all, you know what you wanted to know."

"Certainly," answered Blanche, in a dreamy way.

Monsieur de Pavol learned very soon, to his cost, that if women were not worth a rap, young girls were worth no more, and trampled under foot without wincing the views of a father and' an uncle.

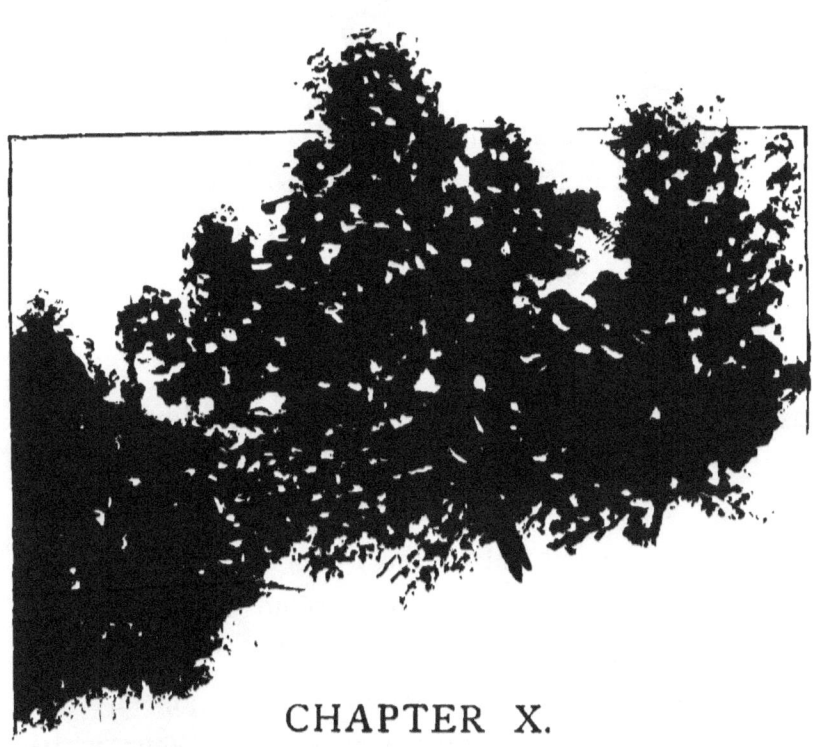

CHAPTER X.

MONDAY morning I got up feeling very happy. I dreamed of Paul de Conprat in the night, and I woke uttering a cry of joy.

The pleasure of putting on for the first time a gown such as I had never owned added still more to my cheerfulness; and when I was dressed, I looked at myself for a long time in silent admiration. Then I set myself to whirling around in an access of exuberant joy, and nearly overturned my uncle in the hall.

"Where are you running to in this fashion, my niece?"

"Into the bedrooms, Uncle, to survey myself in all the mirrors. See how well I look!"

"Not badly, it's a fact."

"Is not my figure pretty in a well-made dress?"

"Charming," answered Monsieur de Pavol, who seemed enchanted at my delight, and who kissed me on both cheeks.

"Ah, Uncle, how happy I am! It is my opinion, as Perrine would say, that the 'extraordinary case' will soon present itself."

Upon that I disappeared and precipitated myself like a water-spout into Juno's room.

"Look!" I cried, spinning around so rapidly that my cousin could see only a whirlwind.

"Be quiet a moment, Reine," she said, with her usual calm. "When will you give up your whirlings? Yes; the dress is very nice."

"Look what a little foot," I said, pushing it forward.

"You inborn coquette!" cried Blanche, laughing. "Who would have thought that such a little savage as you could have already reached such a degree of coquetry?"

"You will see more still," I answered seriously. "I know, you see, that coquetry is an accomplishment, a real accomplishment."

"It is the first time that I have heard it. Who told you? Not your curé, I suppose."

"No, no; but some one who knew perfectly. Is any one beside the De Conprats coming to breakfast, Blanche?"

"Yes; the curé and two of my father's friends."

We installed ourselves in the salon to await our guests; and soon my uncle arrived with the Commandant de Conprat, to whom he presented me.

Mon Dieu! what a handsome face the commandant's was! He had eyes as limpid as those of a child, with mustache and hair as white as snow, and an expression so good, so kindly, that he recalled my curé, though there was not any real resemblance between them. I felt myself drawn to him at once, and I saw that the attraction was mutual.

"A little relative of whom I have heard," he said, taking my hands. "Let me kiss you, my child. I was a friend of your father."

I allowed myself to be embraced with a good grace, not without saying inwardly that I should much prefer to have his son relieve him in this delicate operation.

At last he came; and I would have willingly given my entire *dot*, and my pretty dress to boot, for the right to run to him and embrace him with open arms.

He shook hands with my cousin, and saluted me so ceremoniously that I stood still, quite confused.

"Give me your hand," I said; "you know perfectly well that we are acquainted."

"I was awaiting your good pleasure, Mademoiselle."

"What stupidity!"

"There, there, Reine!" said my uncle, reprovingly.

"A bit of a wild-flower," said the commandant, looking at me in a friendly way, "but a lovely flower, truly."

These words did not succeed in dispelling the irritation which I felt without knowing exactly why, and I remained silent for some time in my corner, watching Monsieur de Conprat, who talked gayly with Blanche. Ah, how charming he seemed, and how my heart beat when I saw again his pleasant smile, his white teeth, and the honest eyes of which I had so often dreamed in my horrid old home! And my aunt, my curé, Suzon, the wet garden, and the cherry-tree in which he had climbed passed across my memory like flying shadows.

Soon I joined in the conversation, and had recovered part of my good-humour when we went into the dining-room.

Seated between the curé and Monsieur de Conprat, I attacked the latter at once.

"Why did you not come back to Buisson?" I said to him.

"I was not the master of my own movements, my cousin."

"You regretted it, at least?"

"Very greatly, I assure you."

"Why, then, did you not shake hands with me when you came?"

"But etiquette required that you should make the first advance, Mademoiselle."

"Ah, etiquette! You did not think of it over there."

"No; we met under peculiar circumstances, and were out of the world, that is certain," he answered, smiling.

"Does the world hinder one from being friendly?"

"No, not exactly; but the proprieties often repress an outburst of friendship."

"It is very silly!" I said shortly.

But 1 was well enough satisfied with the explanation to recover all my spirits. Nevertheless, in talking with him, I perceived that he did not attach the same importance as I to what he had said to me at Buisson. But I was so happy to see him, and to speak with him, that at the moment this little misgiving passed through my mind without impairing its confidence.

"Monsieur de Conprat says that there will be a number of balls in the month of October."

"I am delighted," answered Juno.

"You will teach me how to dance?" I said, dancing already on my chair.

"I demand the office of instructor!" cried Paul de Conprat.

"Paul is an accomplished dancer," said the commandant; "all the ladies like to waltz with him."

"And, besides, he is charming," I added with unction.

The commandant and his son laughed; the curé and my uncle's two friends looked at me smilingly, nod-

ding their heads paternally. But Monsieur de Pavol's
face assumed a displeased expression; and my cousin
raised her eyebrows, — an action peculiar to her when
something displeased her, and an action so full of
disdain that I had the painful impression of having
said something silly.

After dinner we walked in the wood. I had
recovered my cheerfulness, and talked without stopping, amusing myself with imitating the look and
accent of one of our guests whose absurdities struck
me.

"Reine, how badly you have been brought up!"
said Blanche.

"He speaks this way," I answered, pinching my
nose to imitate my victim's voice.

Monsieur de Conprat laughed; but Juno wrapped
herself in an imposing dignity which did not trouble
me the least in the world.

There was a moment when I was beside him, while
my cousin walked on before with a nonchalant air. I
noticed that he watched her closely.

"How beautiful she is, isn't she?" I said to him
in the innocence of my heart.

"Lovely, perfectly lovely!" he answered in a
suppressed voice which made me start.

A doubt and a presentiment crossed my mind; but
at sixteen impressions of this kind take flight and
disappear like the butterflies which flutter about us,

and I was in a state of foolish gayety until our guests said farewell to Monsieur de Pavol.

When they had gone, my uncle retired to his study, and sent for me.

"Reine, you have been ridiculous."

"How, pray, Uncle?"

"One does not say to a young man that he is charming, my niece."

"But it was because I found him so, Uncle."

"All the more reason not to say it."

"What!" I exclaimed, nonplussed. "Then ought I to say that I found him the reverse of charming?"

"You ought not to touch on the subject. Have what opinions you please, but keep them to yourself."

"But it is very natural to say what one thinks, Uncle."

"Not in the world, my niece. Half of the time it is necessary to say what you do not think, and to conceal what you do."

"What a frightful principle!" I exclaimed in horror. "I shall never be able to put it in practice."

"You will learn to; but in the mean time observe the rules of etiquette."

"That everlasting etiquette!" I exclaimed, going out of the room in a bad humour.

That night in dreaming at my window, as I had taken up the custom of doing, my musings were troubled by an indefinite disquiet which I could not well define. I thought over the day, awaited with such impatience; and I could not conceal from myself that things had not gone as I had wished. What had I expected? I did not know; but I talked to myself a long time to convince myself that Monsieur de Conprat was in love with me, and my peroration was followed by a feeling of foreboding.

Nevertheless, the next day my uneasiness had disappeared; but in the afternoon I received a long letter from my curé,—a letter filled with good advice, and ending thus:—

"Petite Reine, your letter has come to console and delight me in my solitude. Do not fail to write me, I pray you. I do not know how to get on without you, and I do not dare to go to Buisson, for fear of weeping like a child. I reproach myself for my selfishness, for you are happy; but, as says the Scripture, the flesh is weak, and my *presbytère*, my duties, and my prayers have not been able to comfort me.

"Farewell, dear, good little child; my last word to you shall be,—Distrust your imagination."

And this sentence produced a disagreeable impression on my already depressed spirits.

CHAPTER XI.

I HAD been installed for three weeks at Pavol; and my uncle asserted that I was so improved in appearance that it would be impossible for the curé to recognize me if he met me. He compared me to a perennial plant which grows well in a thankless soil, because it comes of good stock, but whose beauty develops all at once and incredibly when it is transplanted to a congenial earth.

When I looked into the glass, I had proof that my brown eyes had a new brilliancy, that my lips were ruddier, and that my dark skin was acquiring rosy and delicate tones which awoke in me a lively satisfaction.

Nevertheless, a few days after the breakfast of which I have spoken, I discovered, without a shadow of doubt, that in my great simplicity I was thoroughly deceived in believing that Monsieur de Conprat was in love with me. But I had never been a pessimist, and I called in my logic to console me. I said to myself that of necessity all hearts could not be constructed alike; that some yield instantly, while others must ponder and consider well before taking fire; that if Monsieur de Conprat did not love me, he would some day or other, because it was clear that there was an actual resemblance between our respective tastes and characters. So that although the deception had been a great one, my peace of mind for many days was not seriously affected. And I expanded in this spot so congenial to my tastes; I basked in my happiness like a lizard in the sun.

My cousin was very musical. The commandant, who was devoted to music, came to Pavol often during the week, and his son regularly came with him. The door was always open to him, because of his youthful intimacy with Blanche, and the ties of kinship which united the two families. Furthermore, my uncle saw this intimacy with pleasure, because, with the approval of the commandant, and notwithstanding his diatribes on marriage, he wished very much to marry his daughter to Monsieur de Conprat, finding, with sufficiently good reason, that he represented an "extraordinary case."

I learned of this project later on, at the same time with other facts which I should have discovered easily if I had had more experience.

The gentlemen usually came to breakfast. Paul, endowed with the appetite you know of, ate heartily, and took a bite at three o'clock. After that, if we were alone, Blanche gave me a dancing lesson while he played with animation a waltz of her composition. Sometimes he was the teacher; my cousin took her place at the piano; the commandant and my uncle watched us with a jovial air; and I spun around in the arms of Monsieur de Conprat with a joy unspeakable. Ah, what happy days!

We made no plan without his sharing it. His contagious cheerfulness, his considerate disposition, and the genius for organization and droll invention which he possessed in the highest degree, made him a charming companion, brightened our existence, and increased my love. Adroit, ingenious, and obliging, he was good for everything, and knew how to do everything. If we broke a watch or a bracelet, or no matter what, we would say, Blanche and I, "If Paul comes to-day, he will mend it."

He painted a good deal, and often brought us his productions. It is the only point on which I could never agree with him. I had an inveterate antipathy for the arts; but, above all, for music, because that wretched etiquette forbade me to stop my ears, while it is easy not to look at a picture or to turn one's back on it. Sometimes, when Monsieur de Conprat played dance music, I listened willingly and for a long time; but it was he in the music that I loved, and not the music itself. I note this sentiment in passing, because one day I analyzed it, and the analysis led me to a terrible discovery.

"Why paint the trees, Cousin?" I would say. "The ugliest tree is vastly better than these little green dabs which you put on your canvas."

"Is that the way you understand art, young cousin?"

"Do you not think that Juno is a thousand times more beautiful in reality than in her portrait?"

"Yes, indeed; I know it!"

"And these little blue flowers that you place in the trees, what are they?"

"But that is a bit of sky, Cousin."

I pirouetted, and cried pathetically, —

"O heavens! O trees! O Nature! what crimes are committed in your names!"

My uncle had many friends at V——; he was connected with nearly all the families thereabout, and kept open house. It was seldom that we did not have some guests to breakfast or to dine. It was for me a way of making acquaintance with social customs, and of acquiring, as the curé said, a mental equipoise; but I must say that I acquired little of this, and that I never reached the point of dissembling my impressions and my thoughts, which were often as ridiculous as impertinent.

My uncle and Juno, rigid on the subject of the proprieties, addressed me certain perfectly intelligible remonstrances, but they might as well have talked to the wind. With a persistence truly lamentable, I never lost an opportunity to commit a blunder or make a foolish speech.

"You were very impolite to Madame A——, Reine."

"How, you hypocritical Juno? I let her see that I did not like her, — that's all."

"It is precisely that which is rude, my niece."

"She is so ugly, Uncle! You see I do not feel drawn toward women. They are so satirical and spiteful, and examine you from head to foot as if you were a strange animal."

"How can you reproach them for being satirical, Reine? You spend your time in noticing people's absurdities, and imitating them."

"Yes, but I am pretty, and everything is permitted me; Monsieur C—— told me so the other day."

"I do not agree with his deduction. But do you not believe that men examine you from head to foot?"

"Yes, but it is with admiration; while women look for faults in my figure, or invent them, if need be. You see, I have already noticed a number of things."

"So it appears, my niece; but try to notice that good manners are a real accomplishment."

When our guests were young men, they devoted themselves to Blanche and me, and I was much entertained; but when they were old — *Dieu!* the politics which always started up, enough to make the head ache. Ah, how they bored me, those politics!

The worthy men would arrive, greatly excited at some misdeeds of the government. They would talk with moderation until some fiery Bonapartist would cry that he would like to shoot all republicans, to strike them with terror. The *naïveté* of the expression would cause a 'laugh and clear the decks of irritation and wild talk. We would throw ourselves head-first into politics, and dabble in them until the end of dinner. All agreed in abominating a republic and republicans; but when each guest would draw from his pocket a little scheme of government which he had been careful to bring with him, they were not long in darting furious glances at one another, and becoming red as tomatoes.

The legitimist wrapped himself in the dignity of his traditions, his reverence for the throne, and his regrets, and considered the imperialist a revolutionist; the latter in his inmost soul considered the legitimist a fool, but politeness not allowing him to express his opinion, he would bawl the louder to make up for it. Then some one would fall afresh upon the republicans, would pile up invectives on them, would transport them, would shoot them, would decapitate them,

would pound them to a jelly; imperialists and legiti-
mists would unite in a common hatred to sweep these
unhappy bipeds from the face of the earth. They
would perorate passionately, gesticulate, save the
country, and grow purple in the face, which did not,
alas! prevent things from going on in their own
sweet way.

My uncle, in the midst of these divagations, would
throw out from time to time a witty remark or one
full of good sense, and would raise the discussion
to a more elevated plane than that of personal inter-
ests and individual sympathies. In no sense a legitimist, and yet having no fixed opinions, he none the
less thought that for nearly a century France had
advanced with her eyes on the ground, and that this
abnormal position would end in making her lose her
equilibrium and fall into some abyss, where she
would be buried.

He laughed at the tricks and the blunders of the
different political parties; but he often felt sick at
heart, which he showed by some humorous remark.
I have never seen him angry; he preserved his tranquillity in the midst of the varied clamours of his
guests, sure, for that matter, of having the last word,
because he saw clearly and far. Nevertheless his antipathies were active; and he detested the republicans. Not that he was too much in earnest to be
impartial; he would have accepted a republic had he

believed it practicable, and he respected the honesty of certain men who strove in good faith for a Utopia.

I have sometimes heard him call our rulers racket-players, comparing the laws which the two chambers bandy to and fro daily to the balls, which the French people, gazing aloft, watched devoutly flying through the air, until they fell on their respectable carti-lages and flattened them entirely. From which I drew, for my own little scheme of government, some deductions which I will mention in their time and place.

Monsieur de Pavol liked conversation and even argument. If he spoke little, he listened with interest. Under a rough exterior he had a wide knowledge, a taste correct, elevated, and delicate, great common-sense, and a really high point of view. He was neither a saint nor a bigot. Like the majority of men, he had, I suppose, his weaknesses and his faults; but he believed in God, in the soul, in virtue, and did not in the least consider unbelief, cavilling, and the spirit of disparagement as evidence of manliness and intelligence. He loved to hear materialists and free-thinkers develop their theories; and his mouth was expressive as he watched his opponent and made his heavy brows meet until they almost entirely hid his eyes. Then he would answer slowly and very quietly, —

"*Morbleu*, Monsieur, I admire you! You have

nearly reached that perfect humility preached by the Evangelist. I am overcome at not being able to follow in your steps; but I have a devil of a pride which always prevents my putting myself on a level with the worm which crawls at my feet, or the pig which wallows in my pen."

Always at war with the municipal council of his commune, he did not love the villagers, and declared that no one is more knavish and rascally than a peasant; so that though he was esteemed and respected, he was not loved. Nevertheless, he gave largely in charity, and offered his services when there was occasion; but he never allowed himself to be duped by artifices and the wiles of adventurers.

In short, though my uncle had never chosen any vocation in life, though he had been neither physician, lawyer, engineer, soldier, diplomat, nor even minister, he did his duty in life in perpetuating sound traditions, in respecting what was worthy of respect, in not allowing himself to be carried away by the "isms" of the day, and in using his influence in the direction of what is good and right, — in a word, my uncle was a man of intelligence, a man of heart, a good man. I loved him dearly; and if he had never talked politics, I should have thought that he had not a fault. In his private life he was amiable. He adored his daughter, and very soon gave me a great share of his affection.

"What frightful things governments are!" I said to Monsieur de Conprat. "They ought to be suppressed; then we should hear no more politics. Two things to suppress, — the piano and politics."

"*Ma foi!* I am rather of your opinion," he answered, laughing.

"Ah! you do not like the piano? But you listen to Blanche rapturously; at least, you have that appearance."

"It is because my Cousin Blanche has a real talent."

This explanation gave me that enervating sensation caused by mosquitoes who sing about a sleeper; they annoy him without entirely spoiling his sleep. The explanation was plainly unplausible, because notwithstanding Juno's talent, I, who did not like the piano, had always a desire to scream or to run away when she played Mozart's or Beethoven's sonatas. They are men, these two, who can boast of having bored humanity! I am heart-broken when I think of their wives!

In the midst of this peaceful life, of my hopes and my little inquietudes, which vanished before a kind word, and the distractions of a way of living so new to me, we reached the end of September. My uncle, with the funereal face of a man being led to the scaffold, made ready to escort us to the balls announced by Monsieur de Conprat.

CHAPTER XII.

I CAN answer for my not having exercised my powers of observation at all at my first ball. Of that evening I recall only a delirious joy, and the foolish things I said, because they cost me a sharp reprimand the next day.

From time to time Juno tapped me on the arm with her fan, and whispered in my ear that I was behaving ridiculously; but it was like beating the air, and I flew off in the arms of my partners, thinking that if the waltz is not allowed in heaven, it is hardly worth while to go there.

Sometimes my cavalier tried to make a little conversation.

"You have not lived in this part of the country long, Mademoiselle?"

"No, Monsieur; about six weeks."

"Where did you live before you came to Pavol?"

"At Buisson, — a frightful place, with a frightful aunt, who is dead, *Dieu merci!*"

"In any case, your name is very well known, Mademoiselle; there was a Chevalier de Lavalle shut up at Mont St. Michel in 1423."

"Indeed! What was he doing there, this chevalier?"

"Why, he defended the place when it was attacked by the English."

"Instead of dancing? What a great simpleton!"

"Is that your appreciation of your ancestors and of heroism, Mademoiselle?"

"My ancestors! I never thought of them. As to heroism, I have no opinion of that."

"What has it done to you, this poor heroism?"

"The Romans were heroic, it seems; and I detest the Romans! But let us waltz instead of talking."

And I tired my partner out.

My happiness reached its height when, in that brilliantly lighted salon, under the eyes of the ladies *en grande toilette*, in the midst of that world from which I had been so far such a little time before, I danced with Monsieur de Conprat. There was no doubt that he danced better than any of the others. Although he was large, and I was very small, his beautiful blond mustache, twisted into a point, caressed my cheek from time to time; and I had certain little temptations of which I will not speak, for fear of scandalizing my neighbour.

Intoxicated with joy and the compliments which buzzed around me, I said all the silly things imaginable and unimaginable; but I made the conquest of all the men, and was the despair of all the young girls.

The cotillon excited my wildest enthusiasm; and when my uncle, who had the air of a martyr in his corner, made us a sign that it was time to go, I called out from one end of the salon to the other:

"Uncle, you shall not take me away except at the point of the bayonet!"

But I had to dispense with bayonets, and follow Juno, who, beautiful and dignified as ever, made haste to obey her father without considering my protestations.

Having returned to my room, I undressed myself calmly enough; but when in my nightdress and just on the point of getting into bed, I was seized with an irresistible craze. I caught up my bolster and began to waltz with it, singing at the top of my lungs.

Juno, whose room was not far from mine, came in, a little frightened.

"What are you doing, Reine?"

"You see perfectly well. I am waltzing."

"*Mon Dieu!* what a child you are!"

"My dear, if the world were wise, it would waltz day and night."

"Come, Reine, it is cold; you will be ill. Get into bed, I beg."

I threw my bolster into a corner, and slipped between my sheets. Blanche seated herself on the bed, and began a harangue. She tried to convince me that self-control in every event of life is a great accomplishment; that everything has a time and place; that, after all, a bolster does not seem a very charming partner, and —

"As to that, I am of your opinion," I said, interrupting her abruptly. "It is only dancers in flesh and blood who amount to anything, and are agreeable, especially when they have mustaches; blond mustaches, for instance. A little mustache which caresses the cheek while one is waltzing, — ah! that is truly deli —"

On this I fell asleep, and did not wake up until the next afternoon at three o'clock.

When I was dressed, Monsieur de Pavol asked me to come to his study. I went at once on this invitation, imagining that my uncle's brain was concocting some lecture. From his solemn air I saw that my surmises were correct; and as I always loved my case as much during lectures as in other circumstances of life, I pushed forward an easy-chair, in which I settled myself comfortably; I crossed my hands in my lap, and closed my eyes in an attitude of profound attention.

At the end of two seconds, hearing nothing, I said:

"Very well, Uncle; go ahead."

"Have the kindness to sit up, Reine, and take a more respectful position!"

"But, Uncle," I said, opening my eyes in astonishment, "I had no intention of being disrespectful! I took a receptive position, the better to listen to you."

"My niece, you will drive me distracted!"

"It is very likely, Uncle," I answered quietly; "my curé told me often that I nearly killed him."

"And do you really think that I wish to go to the Devil because of a little girl who has been badly brought up?"

"In the first place, Uncle, I hope you will never go to the Devil, much as you love that personage; secondly, I should be most unhappy to lose you, because I love you with all my heart."

"Hum! that is most delightful. Will you tell me now why, after my lessons and my counsels, you behaved so improperly last night?"

"Make your charges specific, Uncle."

"That would take too long, because everything you did was badly done; you had the air of a horse broken loose. Among other blunders, when you saw Monsieur de Conprat, you called him by his first name. I was near you, and saw that your partner was greatly astonished."

"I believe him capable of it. He had the air of a goose!"

"I am not a goose, Reine; and I tell you that it was not well-bred."

"But, Uncle, he is our cousin; we see him nearly every day, Blanche and I; we always call him Paul when we speak of him, and even when we speak to him."

"That is allowed in the intimacy of private life, but not in the world, where every one is not supposed to know relationships and connections."

"So it is necessary to act in one way at home and in another in the world?"

"That is what I am trying to tell you, my niece."

"It is hypocrisy, neither more nor less."

"In Heaven's name, be a hypocrite! I ask nothing else. Next, it appears that you told five or six young gentlemen that they were very delightful."

"It's perfectly true!" I cried, in an outburst of sympathy for my partners. "So charming, so polite, so attentive! Then I was confused as to my promises, and was afraid of vexing them."

"Meantime, you vex me greatly, Reine. It is now seven weeks since Blanche and I began to try to make you understand that it is good form to weigh your actions and the expression of your opinions; nevertheless, you seize every occasion to say or do some stupid thing. You have intelligence; you are coquettish;

unhappily for me, you have a face ten times too pretty, and —"

"That is something like!" I interrupted delightedly. "How I love lectures!"

"Reine, do not interrupt me; I am speaking seriously."

"Come, Uncle, let us reason. The first time you saw me you said, 'You are devilish pretty!'"

"Very well, my niece?"

"Very well, Uncle; you see clearly that one cannot always repress a first impulse."

"It is possible; but you ought to try, and, above all, to listen to me. Notwithstanding your extreme youth and your slight figure, you have the air of a woman; try to have the dignity of one."

"The dignity!" I said, astonished. "What for?"

"How! What for?"

"I do not understand, Uncle. Would you preach dignity to me when the government has so little?"

"I do not catch the connection. What is this new freak?"

"But, Uncle, you assert that the government passes its time in playing at rackets. For a government, frankly, this is undignified. Why should private individuals be more dignified than ministers and senators?"

My uncle laughed.

"It is difficult to scold you, Reine; you slip through

the fingers like an eel. But be that as it may, I assure you that if you are not willing to listen to me, you shall go no more into society."

"Oh, Uncle, if you did such a thing as that you would deserve the tortures of the Inquisition!"

"The Inquisition being abolished, I shall not be tortured. But you must obey me; be certain of that. I do not wish my niece to acquire habits and manners which, though endurable at her age, would later on make her pass for — hum!"

"For what, Uncle?"

Monsieur de Pavol had a violent fit of coughing.

"Hum! for a woman brought up in the backwoods or some such place."

"Such a description of me would not be so foolish. Buisson and the backwoods are very much alike."

"In short, my niece, make up your mind that I am speaking seriously. Go, and think it over."

This time I realized that I could not trifle with so serious a reprimand. I shut myself up in my room, where I sulked for twenty-eight and a half minutes, during which time I felt springing up in my heart a praiseworthy desire to make acquaintance with self-control.

CHAPTER XIII.

I LEARNED speedily that sometimes proverbs do not belie their reputation for wisdom; that in certain cases to will is to do; and that with a little effort on my part, I was able to put in practice my uncle's suggestions. I do not mean to say that I committed no more blunders, — oh, no, they still came often enough, — but I succeeded in becoming more sedate and in acquiring comparatively quiet ways.

In fact, though my uncle had reproved me, it was rather, as he himself said, with an eye to the future, for I found myself in a place where my words and deeds were judged with the greatest indulgence, — a place full of courtesy, consideration, and kindly traditions, in which, without my suspecting it, I had a goodly number of relatives and connections.

Thanks to my name, my beauty, and my *dot*, many
of my sins against the proprieties were forgiven me.
I was the spoiled child of the dowagers, who repeated
with delight stories of my grandparents, my great-
grandparents, and sundry ancestors whose doings
must have been remarkable to make these amiable
marquises speak of them with so much warmth. I
discovered with satisfaction that ancestors are of some
use in life, and that they hide with their dusty shields
the pertness and whims of youthful descendants who
have come out of the backwoods.

I was the spoiled child of prospective husbands, who
saw my *dot* shine in my beautiful eyes; the spoiled
child of my partners in the dance, because my coquetry
amused them; and I confess very, very low, that I felt
a great delight in laying waste their hearts, and in
turning certain heads into weathercocks.

Oh, Coquetry, what a charm lies hidden in every
letter of thy name!

The taste for it must have been inborn with me,
for after two or three evenings, I knew its details,
its shades, and its wiles.

I should like to be a preacher simply to preach
coquetry to my audience, and to refuse absolution to
my penitents so lacking in judgment as not to give
themselves up to this charming pastime. I should
not perhaps remain long in the bosom of the Church;
but in my brief career I think that I should make

some converts. I pity men who, thinking they know everything, are ignorant of the choicest, the most delicate of pleasures. In my eyes they lead the life of a simpleton, or at best that of a pumpkin.

While I was all animation, and was overturning all hearts, Blanche kept on her way, lovely and haughty, too sure of her beauty to take any trouble, too digni- fied to descend to the excitements and the wiles which delighted me.

Nevertheless, when my first effervescence had sub- sided, I was not long in noticing that Monsieur de Conprat took a very long time to fall in love with me. He saw me under all circumstances, — in full dress, in *demi-toilette*, coquettish, serious, sometimes melan- choly, though rarely, I must confess; and notwith- standing all these varied phases, which prevented an attachment to me being monotonous, not only did he not declare himself, but he seemed really to treat me as a child. My curé's remark, "Make up your mind that he takes you for a little girl of no consequence," began to trouble me greatly.

In spite of my coquetry, my amusements, and my numberless distractions, my love had never changed for an instant. No doubt the excitements of my life prevented my thinking of it constantly, and that ex- plains my long blindness; but I never expected to find a man more charming than Paul de Conprat. And yet, in the court which pressed about me, there were

many suitors who actually resembled the heroes of
Walter Scott whom I had so greatly admired. I often
asked myself how my stout hero, with his cheerful
face and his wonderful appetite, had been able to
affect me so astonishingly when I was under the influence of imaginary personages so little like him.
This is a psychological subject which I shall leave
to the consideration of philosophers, for, as to myself, I have no time to stop; I state the fact, I make
my bow to philosophy, and I pass on.

The 25th of October we had our last dance, in a
château situated near Pavol. I put on a light blue
dress with ornaments in my black hair, which was
coquettishly arranged. I was particularly pretty, and
that night I had a wild success, — a success so
assured that during the following week five offers of
marriage were made to my uncle for me; but I was
restless, feverish, uneasy, and, contrary to my custom,
did not enjoy the infatuation caused by my beauty.

I awaited Monsieur de Conprat impatiently in order
to watch him with my own eyes, which were beginning
to be opened. He generally came very late with three
or four young men, composing the smart set of the
neighbourhood. These gentlemen, being *blasé* from
their earliest youth, and finding it extremely fatigu-
ing, laborious, and heart-rending to dance with pretty
women, secured a few partners with a bored, nonchalant and almost impertinent air, except Paul de Con-

prat, who was too good and too natural not to dance with the satisfaction which the circumstances called for. Sometimes, I must say, my enthusiasm dispelled the *ennui* of these unfortunate victims of experience, as a warm sun dissipates a light mist. I knew so well how to rouse them, to raise their spirits, to make them veer with every breath of my caprice, that my uncle said, "The deuce is in her!"

Evil to him who evil thinketh.

I noticed with vexation that Paul waltzed with Blanche often, while he seldom asked me, and then without ceremony or eagerness. I redoubled my coquetry to attract his attention, but what difference did it make to him? His thoughts and his heart were far from me; and I took refuge in a distant corner, refusing positively to dance.

For a few seconds I hid myself in the curtains which separated the large salon from a boudoir where a number of ladies were sitting; and there I overheard the conversation of two excellent dowagers of whom I had made a conquest.

"Reine is delightful this evening; she is the greatest success, as she always is."

"Blanche de Pavol is more beautiful, though."

"Yes; but she has less charm. She is a haughty queen, and Mademoiselle de Lavalle the adorable little princess of fairy stories."

"Princess is the right word for her; she comes of

a family of princes, and what would shock one in others is charming in her."

"They say that the marriage of her cousin with Monsieur de Conprat is arranged."

"I have heard so."

For some seconds, orchestra, dowagers, waltzers, executed before me a dance without name; and to escape falling I clung to the hangings in which I was shrouded.

When I recovered from my shock, the brilliant salon seemed to me hung with thick *crêpe*.   To Juno's great surprise I begged her to go home at once, without waiting for the cotillon.

As we returned to Pavol, I kept saying to myself, "It is not true; I am sure that it is not true!   Why should I take it so much to heart?"

But I undressed myself in tears, with the feeling that a great trouble was coming upon me.

Still, as nothing is more variable than one's spirits at sixteen, the next day I began to hope again, and to consider the talk of these ladies as idle gossip.   I resolved to watch Monsieur de Conprat; and I was in a condition of mind in which the slightest sign would substantiate my suspicions, though they were past and fleeting.

In the afternoon of this ill-omened day we were all in the salon.   The commandant and my uncle were having a game of chess.   Blanche was playing a sonata of Beethoven; and I, stretched in a chair, watched, under my half-closed eyelids, the attitude and expression of Paul de Conprat. Seated near the piano, a little behind Juno, he listened with a serious air, without taking his eyes off her. I knew that this serious expression was unnatural, and showed that he was bored. I was confirmed in my opinion by noticing that he tried to suppress certain little unseasonable yawns. It was then that I suddenly recalled my own pleasure when he played dance music. I realized that I did not love the airs, but the player, and that he had precisely the same feeling. He did not care for Beethoven, but he was in love with Blanche, and things personally uncongenial pleased him in the woman he loved.

Juno finished her frightful sonata; and Paul said to her with an enthusiasm of which I knew the hidden motive, —

"What a master Beethoven was! You interpret him perfectly, Cousin."

"You yawned!" I cried, springing to my feet so suddenly that the chess-players gave a tremendous growl.

"I thought you were asleep, Reine!"

"No, I was not asleep; and I say that Paul yawned while you were playing your wretched Beethoven."

"Reine dislikes music so much," said my uncle, "that she ascribes to others her own feelings."

"Yes, yes! My feelings have made me a charming discovery," I answered in a trembling voice.

"What is the matter with you, Reine? You are out of
humour because you did not sleep enough last night."

"I am not out of humour, Juno, but I detest hypocrisy; and I repeat, maintain, and will maintain to the
very death that Paul yawned, and yawned a second
time."

After this outburst I fled with the calm of a whirlwind, leaving the occupants of the salon plunged in
astonishment.

I shut myself up in my room, and paced back and
forth, cursing my blindness and thumping myself on
my head with my fist, after the fashion of Perrine
when she was perplexed; but thumping the head
with the fist, aside from its disturbing the brain, has
never been of use as a remedy for unhappy love, and
absolutely discouraged, I fell into an easy-chair,
where I remained a long time, thoroughly chilled
and miserable.

As in all cases of this sort, I recalled words and
occurrences which I said to myself ought to have
enlightened me times without number. My chief
feeling, among many other very confused ones, was
that of intense anger; and my pride awaking, great
and sore, made me swear that no one should perceive my trouble. I was sincere in this, and firmly
believed that it would be easy for me to dissemble

my feelings, although I had been accustomed to hurl them at people's heads.

I was passing through one of those moments of irritation when the most placid individual feels a violent desire to strangle some one or to break something. The nerves, which cannot be relieved by tears, feel the need of some relaxation; and I seized my little terra-cotta men, whose grimaces and smiles seemed to me all at once odious and ridiculous. I hurled them straightway through the window, experiencing a bitter pleasure in hearing them break on the gravel of the walk.

But my uncle, who was passing, received one on his venerable head, happily protected by a hat, and finding the performance outside all the laws of etiquette, uttered an expressive exclamation, —

"What devil's play are you at there, my niece?"

"I am throwing my little men out of the window, Uncle," I answered, approaching the casement, from which I had kept at some distance in order to hurl my projectiles with more force.

"Is that a reason for breaking my head?"

"A thousand pardons, Uncle; I did not see you."

"Have you suddenly gone crazy, my niece? Why do you break all your *bibelots?*"

"They set my teeth on edge, Uncle; they put me out of patience; they make me nervous! There, that's the last of them!"

I hurled five at the same time, and closing the window abruptly, left Monsieur de Pavol to storm against nieces, their whims, and his disordered walk.

That night he lectured me, but I heard absolutely unmoved that miserable lecture, which, in the midst of my serious anxieties, produced no more effect than a soap-bubble breaking on my head.

After dinner I went to look at my little terra-cotta men, which were lying piteously on the walk. Broken! pulverized!—exactly like my illusions and my happiness, which I believed lost forever.

CHAPTER XIV.

M Y lack of perspicacity may perhaps seem astonishing; but who is there, who, without the excuse of my sixteen years, has not given, at some time in his life, proofs of the most inconceivable blindness? I should like to know if there exists a man who does not consider himself a fool for not having seen a thing for a long time, although it was plainly visible. Ah, it is easy to talk of clearsightedness, and as easy to show it, when a thing is under one's —

It was a veritable torture now for me to watch Monsieur de Conprat, to note all the delicate attentions he showed Blanche, knowing perfectly what was the hidden motive. How I wept in secret! But never, I believe, did I feel any great jealousy of

Blanche. *Mon Dieu*, no! I was a little thing who loved sincerely and deeply; there was not the shadow of bitterness in my love. I was, however, in a constant irritation at Monsieur de Conprat. He was the scapegoat upon whom I vented my ill-humour, my heart-ache, and my bitterness; as a matter of course, I never stopped teasing him and saying tart things. Then I would take refuge in my room, where I would stride to and fro, saying to myself, —

"What an intelligent thing it is to fall in love with a woman whose character is so little like your own! He so gay, so talkative, — as talkative as I am, really! and she sedate, silent, a worshipper of etiquette, while he is sometimes bored by it, — I see it clearly. We are so alike! Why has he not seen it? But Blanche is as good as she is beautiful; he has known her a long time; and, after all, love is not its own master —"

But these excellent reasons did not console me in the least. I went to bed sobbing, and even sometimes sobbed in the night; and notwithstanding my firm resolve to hide my feelings, by the end of a fortnight the family and *habitués* of Pavol were astonished at my strange caprices.

In the morning I would be light-hearted almost to laughter; in the evening I would take my place at the table with a sombre mien, and would not open my lips during the meal.

This silence, so contrary to my habits, disquieted Monsieur de Pavol greatly.

"What is passing through your little brain, Reine?"

"Nothing, Uncle."

"Are you bored? Would you like to travel?"

"Oh, no, no, Uncle! I should be very sorry to leave Pavol."

"If you still wish to marry, my niece, you are free to do so. I am not a tyrant. Do you regret the refusals to the proposals which have been following one another for some time?"

"No, Uncle; I have given up my idea. I do not wish to marry."

These unhappy proposals added to my troubles. I could not hear of marriage without wanting to weep. Though Monsieur de Pavol did not urge me to accept, he made me see the advantages of each offer, and insisted mildly that I should at least make the acquaintance of my suitors. He would even have easily enough passed them as "extraordinary cases;" and among the numberless discoveries which I was making every day, my uncle's inconsistency was not the least astonishing. At the bottom of his heart I believe that he was a little frightened at the charge of a soul, which had fallen upon him. But he left me entirely free, and was satisfied with my reasons for refusing certain offers, although they had neither head nor tail.

"Why did you say so often that you were eager to marry, Reine?" Blanche asked me.

"I will not marry until I have found what I wish."

"Ah! and what do you wish?"

"I do not know yet," I answered chokingly.

Blanche took my face in her two hands and looked at me closely.

"I would like to read your thoughts, little Reine. Do you love any one? Is it Paul?"

"I swear that it is not," I said, escaping from her embrace. "I do not love any one, and when I do, you shall know it at once."

If death were not such a frightful thing, I am sure that one could have killed me then before I would have acknowledged my love for a man who loved another woman, and this woman my cousin. Happily it was a question of neither the stake nor the guillotine, the sight of which would probably have destroyed my stoicism.

"I am doing as you are doing, Blanche, — I am waiting."

"I am not the same success as my little savage from Buisson," she said, smiling. "Five proposals at once!"

"Don't speak to me of it any more, I beg; it tires me, bores me, and wears me out."

Unhappily a sixteenth suitor, uniting in himself qualities the most rare, the most extraordinary, the most perfect, placed himself all at once in the ranks

of my adorers. Alas! I reaped what I had sown, because on entering society I had taken pains to say to every one that I meant to marry as soon as possible.

My uncle summoned me, and we had a long talk together.

"Reine, Monsieur Le Maltour desires the honour of marrying you."

"Great good may it do him, Uncle!"

"Does he please you?"

"Not at all!"

"Why not? Give me some reasons, good reasons; those the other day, for the offers you refused off-hand, were worth nothing."

"Your suitors were not presentable, Uncle."

"Let us see: Monsieur de P—— was excellent."

"Oh, a man of thirty! Why not a patriarch?"

"And Monsieur C——?"

"A frightful name, Uncle!"

"Monsieur de N——, a young fellow of excellent parts and very intelligent?"

"I counted his hairs. He had not over fourteen; and he only twenty-six years old."

"Ah! and little D——?"

"I do not like dark men. Besides, he is a perfect nonentity. Once married, he would adore his figure, his cravats, and my *dot*, that's all!"

"I give you up; but to come back to the Baron Le Maltour, what do you object to in him?"

"A man who only danced square dances with me because I did not waltz *à trois temps!*" I cried with. indignation.

"A real grievance! Reine, I repeat that I think it absurd to marry so young; but notwithstanding your *dot* and your beauty, perhaps you will never again have an offer like this. He is a thorough gentleman, and I have the best reports as to his morals and his character; he has an immense fortune, a title; his family is honourable and very ancient."

"Ah, yes; ancestors! that is what Blanche said," I interrupted disdainfully. "I have a horror of ancestors, Uncle."

"Why so?"

"People whose only idea was to fight and get their heads broken. What idiocy!"

"Very well! I know that the registrar of the court at V—— thinks you charming. He has no ancestors; would you like him to be told that for that reason Mademoiselle de Lavalle is disposed to marry him?"

"Do not laugh at me, Uncle; you know perfectly well that I am patrician to my finger-tips," I answered, seizing the occasion to admire my hand and the ends of my taper fingers.

"That is what I thought, if your appearance did not deceive me. Now, my niece, listen to me. You do not know Monsieur Le Maltour well enough to form an opinion of him; and I must insist on your seeing him a number of times before giving a final answer. I am going to write Madame Le Maltour that the decision rests with you, and that I authorize her son to present himself at Pavol whenever it shall seem good to him."

"Very well, Uncle; it shall be as you wish."

Five minutes after, I was wandering in the wood, a prey to the most violent agitation.

"Ah, that is it!" I said, biting my handkerchief to stop my sobs; "he shall have a pleasant reception, this Maltour. I will give him four days to vanish out of my life. And my uncle, who sees nothing, who understands nothing!"

I was mistaken. My uncle, notwithstanding my sudden attempts at dissembling, saw very clearly, but he acted wisely. He could not prevent Monsieur de Conprat from loving his daughter, and abandon the dream in which he and the commandant had indulged so long. Besides, thoroughly convinced that my feeling had little depth, and that there was much of child's play in it, he fancied that the best way to cure this caprice was to turn my thoughts toward a man who, in loving me, would make me love him, according to the axiom, Love begets love.

His reasoning would have been perfect had he not been mistaken in his premises.

Two days later Madame Le Maltour and her son arrived at Pavol, smiles on their lips and hope in their glances. The excellent lady said a hundred amiable things to me, to which I responded with a Jesuitical scowl.

The baron was a good soul — allow me, I do not mean to say by that, that he was stupid, not at all. He was intellectual and witty; but he was only twenty-three years old. He was bashful and very much in love, — a final peculiarity which did not unlock his wits, but which it would be bad taste in me to reproach him with.

The next day he came to see us without his mother, and made an effort to talk to me.

"Are you sorry that there are no more balls, Mademoiselle?"

"Yes," answered I, in a tone as supercilious as that of Suzon.

"Did you have a good time the other day, at the ——s'?"

"No!"

"It was brilliant, though. What a pretty dress you wore! Do you like blue?"

"Evidently, since I wore it."

Monsieur Le Maltour coughed discreetly, to keep up his courage.

"Are you fond of travel, Mademoiselle?"

"No."

"You surprise me; I should have thought you loved adventure and change of scene."

"How silly! I am afraid of everything."

The conversation went on for some time in this fashion. Disconcerted by my curtness and the interest with which, in the most impertinent way in the world, I watched the performances of a fly who was walking on the arm of my chair, the baron rose, a trifle red, and cut short his visit.

My uncle escorted him to the garden gate, and came back in a rage to find me.

"This cannot go on, Reine! You are rude to me as well as to this poor fellow, who is bashful, and whom you disconcert absolutely. Monsieur Le Maltour is not a man to be treated like a puppet, my niece. No one will oblige you to marry him, but I wish you to be polite and amiable. Heaven knows you have a glib tongue when you wish! Try to have it to-morrow. Monsieur Le Maltour will breakfast here."

"Very good, Uncle; I will talk, have no fear."

"Don't talk foolishly either."

"I will get my inspiration from science, Uncle," I answered majestically.

"How? From —"

"Do not worry; I will do as you wish, — I will talk without stopping."

"That is not the point, my niece —"

But I left my uncle to confide his thought to the furniture of the salon, and ran into the library to find what was necessary to carry out the idea which had come into my head. I took away with me Malebranche's Philosophy, and a work on Tartary.

Malebranche nearly produced a delirium; and I abandoned him to devote myself to Tartary, which had more to offer me. I studied some pages hard until midnight, grumbling at and anathematizing the inhabitants of Bokhara, who wore such strange names. I succeeded, however, in mastering some details about the country and many strange words of the significance of which I was entirely ignorant. I went to bed, rubbing my hands.

"We shall see," I said to myself, "if Le Maltour will withstand this experience. Ah, my worthy uncle, I will get the best of him, be sure of that; and in a few hours I shall be rid of this intruder."

The next day he presented himself with the pleasing and awkward air of a man who is treading on needles; but I received him so graciously that he was soon at his ease, and Monsieur de Pavol's anxiety disappeared.

The De Conprats and the curé breakfasted with us. It made my heart ache to watch Paul talking gayly with Blanche, while I was condemned to undergo the bashful attentions of Monsieur Le Maltour, whose fine figure wore on my nerves.

"I have changed my opinion since yesterday," I
said to him suddenly. "I am very fond of travel."

"I share your taste, Mademoiselle; it is the most
intellectual of pleasures."

"You have travelled?"

"Yes, a little."

"Do you know the Ruddars, the Schakird-Pische, .
the Usbecs, the Tadjics, the Mollahs, the Dehbas-
chi, the Pendja-Baschi, the Alamanes?" I said, all
in a breath, confounding race, class, and rank.

"Who are all they?" demanded the astounded
baron.

"What! have you never been in Tartary?"

"No, never."

"Never been in Tartary!" I exclaimed scornfully.
"At least you know Nasr-Oullah-Bahadin-Khan-Melic-
el-Mounemin-Bird-Blac-Bloc and the Devil?"

I added some syllables at my own pleasure to the
name of Nasr-Oullah, to produce more effect, believing that the spirit of this worthy man would not rise
from the tomb to reproach me.

My uncle and his guests bit their lips to keep from
laughing.

Monsieur Le Maltour looked really frightened; and
Blanche cried, —

"Are you crazy, Reine?"

"No, not in the least! I was asking Monsieur
whether he shared my liking for Nasr-Oullah, — a

man who, it appears, had all the vices. He passed his time in cutting his fellow-creatures' throats, in throwing ambassadors into dungeons where he left them to rot; in short, he was endowed with energy, and was never timid, — a horrible fault, in my opinion. And his country! What a lovely country! All diseases raged there; and there is where I should send my husband. Consumption, small-pox, vomitings that last six months, ulcers, leprosy, a worm called rischta, which gnaws you; to get rid of it, one — "

"Enough, Reine, enough; let us breakfast in peace."

"What would you have, Uncle? I find myself drawn to Tartary. And you?" I said to Monsieur Le Maltour.

"What you say is indeed not very encouraging, Mademoiselle."

"For those who have no blood in their veins," I answered scornfully. "When I am married, I shall go to Tartary."

"*Dieu merci!* you will not be your own master, my niece."

"Be very sure that I will, Uncle. I shall always go to my own head, and not mind my husband. For that matter, I will take him to Bokhara to be eaten by worms."

"How! to be eaten by — " murmured the baron, timidly.

"Yes, Monsieur; you have heard correctly. I said 'eaten by worms,' because in my eyes the most charming position in life is that of a widow!"

High and puissant Baron Le Maltour, though of a gallant race, could not resist this. Realizing the hidden meaning in my *tartaric* caprices, he departed and did not return.

My uncle was angry, but I did not trouble myself in the least. I pirouetted, and said to him in a sententious tone, —

"Uncle, who wishes an end, contrives the means."

CHAPTER XV.

I HAD kept my promise to the curé, and had written him very regularly twice a week. The habit seemed so sweet and consoling to him that when all at once I interrupted the regularity of my correspondence, he was plunged in grief and anxiety.

Absorbed in my troubles, I remained a fortnight without giving a sign of life; then, yielding to his urgent entreaties, I sent him letters like this:—

"Man is a stupid creature, Monsieur le Curé,—I am getting to find that out. What is your opinion, my curé? I embrace you,—in defiance of all the proprieties."

Or,—

"Ah, my poor curé, I am afraid I have discovered the source of the cold water of which we were talking three months ago. Happiness does not exist; it is a lure, a myth, anything you will, except reality.

"Adieu; if death did not make us so ugly, I should be glad to die. To die,—yes, my curé, you have read it aright."

He sent me letter after letter.

DEAR DAUGHTER, — What does the tone of your last notes mean? Three weeks ago you seemed so happy in the joy and pride of your social success. No, no, little Reine; happiness is not a myth, — it shall be yours. But at the moment imagination has possession of you, carries you away, and hinders you from seeing accurately. You have not followed my advice, Reine; you have made too great bonfires, have you not? Poor little child, come to see me, and we will talk over together what is in your mind.

I replied to him, —

MONSIEUR LE CURÉ, — Imagination is a fool; life is a thing of shreds and patches, and the world an old rag, dazzling enough when seen from afar, but good only at best to hang in a cherry-tree to frighten the birds. I should like to enter La Trappe, my dear curé! If I were sure that I should be allowed to waltz from time to time with charming men such as I know, I should certainly take refuge there and bury my youth and beauty; but I believe that kind of amusement is not allowed under the rules. Advise me on this point, Monsieur le Curé, and make up your mind that you are simply an optimist in pretending that happiness is real and will fall to my lot. You lead the life of a rat in a cheese. I do not mean that you are selfish; but you do not know the catastrophes that can overtake those who live in the world. I have no more illusions, my curé. I am a little old woman, stunted, shrunken, and shrivelled, — mentally, I mean, because I am prettier than ever,— a little old woman, who no longer believes in anything or hopes for anything, and who says to herself that the world is very stupid to go on with its revolutions when her joys and dreams are dissipated, pulverized, and reduced to imperceptible atoms. My inner man, if one could strip off its carnal covering, — which deceives the observer's eye, I admit, — my inner man, I say, is nothing but a skeleton, a dead tree, completely dead, without sap, and leafless, and holding toward heaven its great rigid, emaciated arms. Can the mind destroy the body, Monsieur le Curé? I tremble at the thought. To have no illusions left at sixteen, is not that terrible?

Au revoir, my old curé.

Two days after sending this letter, which ought to have given the curé a sufficiently melancholy idea of my state of mind, my uncle decided that we should go to spend an afternoon at Mont St. Michel. That day there was something sinister in the air; I felt it. The night before, the commandant and Monsieur de Pavol had had a long and private interview. Paul seemed uneasy and nervous, and my cousin thoughtful.

My uncle and Juno, who were devoted to Mont St. Michel, did me the honours of the place with complacence; but architecture interested me very little, and besides, I saw everything through the dark veil of a perfectly killing temper.

"How tiring it is to climb all these steps!" I said, whining at each one.

"More than six hundred to scale to reach the top, my cousin."

"I want to stop, then."

"Come, my niece, what the deuce, you haven't the gout?"

And as he climbed the steps trodden by so many generations, my uncle recited to me the history of the mount and the incident of Montgomery.

But how did it concern me,—this Montgomery, these ramparts, this marvellous abbey, these mighty halls, these numberless souvenirs which have slept there for centuries? I should have taken good care not to awaken them, for I was a hundred times more interested in watching the face of the big fellow who was so attentive and so thoughtful for Blanche, and never considered me at all.

What a fool I was not to have seen his love sooner! He went into ecstasies over the smallest stone to please her; and from time to time I cast some black looks at him, which he did not even deign to notice.

"Ah, here we are in the *salle des chevaliers.* Come, Reine, what have you to say to this?"

"I say, Uncle, that if the chevaliers were here, the hall would be charming."

"You don't find it so in itself?"

"Not in the least. I see huge fireplaces and columns with little designs carved at top; but without the chevaliers whose heads one might perhaps turn a little — pooh! it all amounts to nothing."

"I had never thought of that way of looking at feudal architecture," answered my uncle, laughing.

We went through dark passages which frightened me.

"We are going to break our necks," I groaned, clinging tightly to the commandant's arm, while Paul offered his to Blanche.

"You are in trouble, little Reine?" said the commandant to me, in a very low tone.

"You speak like my curé," I answered, greatly moved.

"Come, do you want to confide in me?"

"I have no trouble," I answered chokingly, "and I have no confidence in any one. Suzon told me that men were good for nothing, and I am of Suzon's opinion!"

"Oh, oh!" said the commandant, watching me with so kindly an air that I was afraid of breaking into sobs; "such misanthropy in one so young!"

I did not answer; and as we were reaching a sort of long terrace, I made my escape and ran to hide behind an enormous row of columns. I leaned my head on one of the stones, many hundreds of years old, and wept.

"Ah," I thought, "how right my curé was in telling me a long time, a very long time, ago, that one does not argue with life, one submits. All my logic is good for nothing under these circumstances. How

miserable it is, — *mon Dieu!* how miserable it is to see
one's self treated as a little girl of no consequence! "

And through my tears I looked at those famous
sands, which seemed to me dreary, at the pile whose
height oppressed and made me dizzy; but without
knowing why, I felt a kind of relief in that strange
affinity of Nature, which seemed sad in accord with
my own feelings, and in the contemplation of those
great walls which threw their melancholy shadows
across the earth and the past.

When we were in the train on our way home, my
uncle said to me, —

"Well, Reine, taken all together, what is your feeling about Mont St. Michel?"

"I think, Uncle, that one would die of fear there,
and would catch the rheumatism."

As we drove along the route which led from the
station at V—— to Pavol, I reflected that few things
are stable here below. It was hardly three months
since I passed over the same road, full of happy
dreams, in an intoxication of joyous thoughts about
that future which I believed so beautiful, and now
the way seemed strewn with the débris of my
happiness.

It was quite late when we reached the château;
nevertheless, my uncle took Blanche into his study,
saying that he wished that very evening to have a
serious talk with her.

I went to bed weeping with all my heart, and with the conviction that the sword of Damocles was hanging over my head.

For a long time Juno had been very friendly with me. Every morning she would come and sit on my bed, and we would talk indefinitely. The next day about seven o'clock she came into my room, with a calm and tranquil step, and that charming smile which transfigured her haughty face, and which perhaps I alone knew well.

"Reine," she said to me suddenly, "Paul has proposed for me."

The thread was broken, and the sword of Damocles fell on my breast. How lacking in common-sense was that king to hang so heavy a thing by a simple thread! Does not history call it a hair? It is very likely.

There is no doubt that I was expecting this revelation; but so long as a fact is not proved and accomplished, where is the human being who does not cherish a little hope at the bottom of her heart? I became very pale, so pale that Blanche noticed it, although the room was darkened.

"What is the matter, Reine? Are you ill?"

"A cramp," I murmured feebly.

"I will go and get the ether," she exclaimed, jumping up quickly.

"No, no," I answered, making a violent effort to

recover my pride, which was vanishing into thin air;
"it is over, Blanche, entirely over."

"Have you had this trouble often, Reine?"

"No, only occasionally. It is nothing; don't say
anything more about it."

Blanche passed her hand across her forehead, like
one who tries to drive away an intrusive thought;
but I resumed the conversation in so steady a voice
that she seemed relieved of her anxiety.

"Well, Juno, what do you intend to do?"

"My father says the marriage would meet all his
views, Reine."

"Would you like it?"

"The marriage would suit me evidently; for all
considerations favour it; only I do not love Paul
except as a cousin."

"What fault do you find in him?"

"I find no fault, except that he does not please
me enough. He is a capital fellow, but I do not
love that kind of man. In the first place, he
is not handsome enough; then that abnormal appetite of his is not poetical, you will agree to
that."

"But it is perfectly logical to eat when one is
hungry," I answered, keeping back my tears.

"What would you have? I think that we should
not get on well together."

"Are you going to refuse him, then, Juno?"

"I have asked a month to consider it, little Reine. I am very perplexed, for I dread to disappoint my father. Besides, from certain points of view the match would be all I could wish; and lastly, the man is thoroughly estimable."

"But if you do not love him, Blanche?"

"My father holds that I will love him later, and for that matter that love, so called, is not necessary for marriage and happiness in a home."

"How can you believe a thing like that?" I said, springing up with indignation. "My uncle really has abominable opinions!"

But Blanche answered tranquilly that her father was full of good sense; that she had often noticed that he was seldom deceived in his judgments, and that she was disposed to listen to him.

"Does Paul love you very much, Juno?" I murmured under my breath.

"Yes, and has for some time."

"Did you know it?"

"Of course; a woman always knows such things. And you,—did you not see it?"

"Yes—a little," I answered, sending a backward glance full of melancholy at my stupidity.

Blanche left me after explaining that Paul had delayed asking her hand because he was afraid of being refused.

It was exactly as I thought; and I dressed my-

self feverishly, thinking that under her father's influence she would end by giving her consent.

In her place, I should have said yes in a second,
and a fortnight after I should have been married.

Alas! it was the end of my dreams; and I fell into
a deep depression.

CHAPTER XVI.

I T was arranged that Paul should not come to
Pavol for some time, and though the thing
appeared to me incredible and unheard of, from the
day when she ceased to see him Blanche seemed as
if she had nearly made up her mind to marry him.
We talked of him together constantly; we even dis-
cussed wedding dresses; and I showed a stoic resignation worthy of the men of antiquity.

But this resignation was only on the surface.

My despondency increased; my eyes had black cir-
cles; and I had reached the point of saying to myself
that, life being insupportable away from the man I
loved, the simplest thing to do was to take my departure to the other world.

This plan was obviously a very painful one, but I
clung to it eagerly. I thought over it; I cherished it
with an almost morbid delight. Yet I swear on my

honour that I never had any idea of suffocating my-self or of swallowing poison,— methods of suicide so dear to those of our day. But having read, in I do not know what book, that a young girl had died of grief from an unhappy love-affair, I decided that I would follow her example.

My course of action decided on, and my ill looks confirming my lugubrious thoughts, I considered that it was polite and proper to inform the curé, and that, indeed, I could not die without pressing his hand.

This being determined on, I entered my uncle's study one morning and begged him to let me go to Buisson.

"It would be better to ask the curé to come here, Reine."

"He could not, Uncle; he never has a sou in his pocket."

"It will not be very enlivening for me to take you there, my niece."

"Do not come, Uncle, I beg; you would be dread-fully in the way. I want to go alone with the old housekeeper, if you will let me."

"Do as you wish. My carriage shall take you to C——, where it will be easy to find some convey-ance to carry you to Buisson. When shall you go?"

"To-morrow morning, early, Uncle; I want to sur-prise the curé, and I will sleep at the *presbytère.*"

"Very well; so be it. I will send the carriage for

you in a couple of days; be at C—— day after to-morrow about three."

He watched me closely under his heavy eyebrows, rubbing his chin thoughtfully.

"Are you ill, Reine?"

"No, Uncle."

"Little niece," he said, drawing me to him, "I have almost come to hope that my plans shall not succeed."

I looked at him, thoroughly astonished, because I had always firmly believed that he had seen nothing.

I answered him very coolly that I did not know what he meant; that I was very happy, and that I would pray that all his plans might succeed. He embraced me affectionately, and dismissed me.

I set out, then, the next morning without Blanche, who wished to go with me.

On the way I thought over my uncle's words.

"He knows all," I said to myself. "*Mon Dieu!* how blind I was in my assumptions! But even though Juno's marriage should not take place, what difference could that make to me, since Paul is in love with her? He could not love another person now. I don't understand my uncle."

I did not believe now, any more than before, that one could love several women. Judging from my own feelings, I said to myself that a man could not love twice in his life without presenting to the world a most astonishing phenomenon.

Having thus regulated the heart-throbs of bearded humanity, my thoughts took another direction, and I was filled with delight at the idea of seeing my curé. I resolved to throw myself on his neck, were it only to show my independence and my contempt for conventionalities.

Having reached the *presbytère*, I entered, not by the gate, but through a hole in the hedge which I had known from time immemorial, and advanced on tiptoe toward the window of the parlour, where the curé ought to be just about breakfasting. The window was very low; but I was so small that to look into the room I had to climb on a log which had been rolled against the wall for a seat.

I lifted my head cautiously through the ivy, which made a leafy frame to the casement, and I saw my curé.

He was at the table, and was eating dejectedly. His cheeks had lost some of their colour and their roundness; his thick white hair no longer stood on end, as of old, but lay flat on his head in an inexpressibly melancholy fashion.

"Ah, my poor, good curé!"

I leaped down from the log; I rushed into the *presbytère*, losing my hat as I went, and burst into the parlour like a bomb.

The curé rose with a start. His kindly and good face shone with joy on seeing me; and it was not to break the traditions of etiquette, but in an outburst of genuine affection and of strong feeling, that I threw myself into his arms and wept a long time on his shoulder. I know perfectly that nothing in the world is more contrary to etiquette than to weep on the shoulder of a curé; that my uncle, Juno, and all the dowagers of the land, in spite of my ancestors, would have veiled their faces before a sight so scandalous. But I had been too short a time at the school of self-control to lose my spontaneity. Besides, I am positive that only idiots and unnatural and heartless people believe in never sacrificing the proprieties to real and deep feeling.

"Life is an old rag, my curé,—a miserable old rag," I said, sobbing.

"Have we come to that, dear little daughter, have we really come to that? No, no; it is not possible!"

And the poor curé, who smiled and wept at the same time, looked at me affectionately, stroked my head with his hand, and spoke to me as to a little wounded bird, whose broken wing he would have cured by caresses and kind words.

"Come, Reine, come; calm yourself a little, my dear child," he said, raising me gently.

"You are right," I answered, thrusting my handkerchief into the bottom of my pocket. "For three months I have had self-control preached to me; and I have not profited in the least by the lessons, as

you see. Let us have something to eat, Monsieur le Curé."

I took off my gloves and my cloak; and in one of those reversions of feeling to which I had been subject for some time, I began to laugh, and established myself joyfully at the table.

"We will talk when we have eaten, my dear curé; I am dead with hunger!"

"But I have almost nothing to give you."

"Here are beans,— I adore beans! and home-made bread,— it's delicious!"

"But you did not come alone, Reine?"

"Sure enough; the housekeeper is still sitting in the carriage behind the church. Send for her, Monsieur le Curé, and tell them to pick up my hat, which is walking about the garden."

The good curé went to give the orders, and came back and sat opposite me. While I ate with a capital appetite, notwithstanding my consumption and my troubles, he forgot all about his breakfast, and watched me with an admiration which he strove in vain to hide.

"You find me prettier, do you not, Monsieur le Curé?"

"Yes —a little, Reine."

"Ah, my curé, if I were going to confess, what great sins I should have to tell you of! They are no longer the little sins of old, which you knew so well."

And without ceasing to eat, I told him of all my vain delights, my impressions, my dresses, my new ideas. He laughed, took snuff without stopping, with his old jocund air, and looked at me without in the least thinking of finding fault.

"Am I not on the road to perdition, Monsieur le Curé?"

"I do not think so, my good little child. One must be young when one is young."

"Young, my poor curé! If you could see into the bottom of my heart! I wrote you that I was nothing but a skeleton, and it is really true."

"You do not look it, at all events."

"We will talk together in a moment, Monsieur le Curé, and you will see!"

When I had changed my seat, the servant cleared the table, made a magnificent fire, and we took our places, each in a chimney-corner.

"Come, Reine, let us talk seriously now. What have you to tell me?"

I stretched out my little foot to the blaze, and answered quietly,—

"My curé, I am dying!"

The curé, a little startled, shut with a snap the snuff-box, in which he was about to introduce the ends of his fingers.

"You do not look it, my dear child."

"What! you have not noticed my heavy eyes, my pale lips?"

"Not at all, Reine; your lips are red, and your face is blooming with health. But of what are you dying?"

Before answering, I looked around me, reflecting that I was going to pronounce a word which this modest room had never heard uttered within its wretched walls,—a word so strange that the old clock without a spring, which stood in a corner, and the pious images fastened to the walls, would probably fall on my head in a transport of surprise and indignation.

"Well, Reine?"

"Well, Monsieur le Curé, I am dying of love!"

The clock, the images, the furniture, preserved their immobility; and the curé himself gave only a little jump.

"I was sure of it," he said, running his hands through his hair, which had resumed the bushy ways of happy days,—"I was sure of it. Your imagination has played tricks with you, Reine."

"It is not a question of the imagination, but of the heart, Monsieur le Curé, for I am in love."

"Oh, so young! such a child!"

"Is that any reason? I repeat that I am dying of love for Monsieur de Conprat."

"Ah! it is he, then?"

"Do you take me for a rattlebrain, a thoughtless creature, my curé?" I cried.

"But, little Reine, instead of dying, you would do better to marry him."

"That would be logical, my dear curé, very logical, but, unhappily, I do not please him."

This assertion seemed to him so extraordinary that he remained petrified for some seconds.

"It cannot be possible," he exclaimed in a tone of such conviction that I could not keep from laughing.

"Not only does he not love me, but he loves some one else; he is infatuated with Blanche, and has proposed for her."

I recounted what had been taking place for some time at Pavol,— my discoveries, my blindness, and Juno's indecision. I finished the account with hot tears, for my disappointment was very real.

The curé, who until then had not been able to make up his mind to take my words and troubles seriously, presented the picture of consternation. He drew his chair near mine, took my hand, and tried to reason with me.

"Your cousin is undecided; perhaps the marriage will not take place."

"What difference will that make, since he is in love? One cannot love twice."

"Such a thing has been seen, my little child."

"I cannot believe it; it would be horrible. I am very unhappy, my poor curé."

"Have you spoken to your uncle?"

"No; but he has divined my thoughts. Besides, what would be the use? He could not force Paul to love me and forget his daughter. I would not have him know of my love, I would rather die."

A long silence followed this manifestation of my pride. We looked into the fire like two good little sorcerers who were trying to read the secrets of the future in the flames and the glowing embers.

But flames and embers made no answer, and I was weeping silently, when the curé resumed, with a half-smile,—

"He does not, then, resemble either Francis I. or Buckingham!"

"Ah, Monsieur le Curé," I answered quickly, "if Francis I. or Buckingham were there, they would not have to be entreated to love me, and I should be very happy."

"Hum!" the curé found this answer unorthodox and capable of unpleasant interpretations.

He abandoned at once a subject so bristling with snares, and preached resignation.

"Consider, Reine, how young you are. This trial will pass, and you have a long life before you."

"I have not a resigned nature, my curé; learn that. If I live, I shall never marry; but I shall not live,— I am consumptive, listen!"

And I tried to produce a hollow cough.

"Don't let us joke on that subject, Reine. *Dieu merci!* you are in good health."

"Come," I said, rising, "I see that you will not believe me. Let us take advantage of the fine weather and the few moments I have left of life to go to Buisson, Monsieur le Curé."

We set out briskly for my old home under a pleas-ant November sun infinitely less sweet, less genial, than the affection of my curé, and the sight of his kindly face grown all rosy since my coming. I watched with delight his hair fluttering in the wind, his elastic step, his whole figure, stout and jocund, which I had watched so often through the hall win-dow while the rain whipped the panes and the wind roared and whistled through the dilapidated doors of the old house.

After a visit to Perrine and Suzon, I went through it from top to bottom. Truly, time should not be measured by the number of days that have passed, but by the vividness and the number of events. A very few weeks before I had left this old ruin; and if some one had told me that many years had passed over my head, I should have really believed them.

I dragged the curé into the garden. Poor virgin forest! it recalled unhappy days, yet I was delighted to go all over it.

And then the remembrance of some rapturous hours came into my head,—a remembrance still delightful to me, notwithstanding the bitterness of the misconceptions that had followed a moment of happiness.

"Do you remember, Monsieur le Curé?" I said, pointing out the cherry-tree which Paul had climbed.

"Let us talk of something else, little Reine."

"Is it possible, my dear curé? If you knew how I love him! He has no faults, I assure you!"

Once started on this subject, no power, human or supernatural, could have stopped me, the more that at Pavol I was obliged to hide my feelings. I talked so long that the unhappy curé was entirely dazed.

We passed the evening in conversing and arguing. The curé employed all his oratorical skill to prove to me that resignation is a virtue full of wisdom and easy of acquirement.

"My curé," I answered seriously, "you do not know what love is."

"Believe me, Reine, with a little effort you will forget and easily overcome this trial. You are so young!"

So young!—that was his refrain. Does not one suffer at sixteen as at no matter what age? These old people are astonishing!

On my side I answered, shaking my head,—

"You do not understand, my curé; you do not understand!"

The next morning, while he walked with me in his garden, I said to him,—

"Monsieur le Curé, I had an idea last night."

"Let us have the idea, ma petite."

"I want you to come to the living at Pavol."

"One cannot take another's place, Reine."

"The curate of Pavol is as old as Herod, Monsieur le Curé; he ages fast, and I watch the signs of weakness with a tender solicitude. Would you not like to succeed him?"

"Yes, of course; yet I should be sorry to leave my parish. Thirty-five years have I been here, and I love it now."

"Now! have you not always loved it?"

"No, indeed, Reine; you know how dull it is. Perhaps it has never occurred to you that I have been young. My aspirations were not exactly like yours, my little child; but I should have loved an active life; I should have loved to see and to hear things, for I did not lack intelligence, and I desired the intellectual resources which I have never had. Then, before you came into my life, I had neither affection nor friendship from a soul. But one overcomes vexations and disappointments, Reine, when one really wishes. I was very happy for a long time before you left Buisson; I had forgotten the dreary and evil days of my youth."

The good curé looked before him, a little thoughtfully; and I, who had never imagined, seeing him so light-hearted and contented, that he had suffered in

his time, was touched by his resignation so real, so
sweet, and so free from rancour.

"You are a saint, my curé!" I said, taking his
hand.

"*Chut!* Don't talk nonsense, dear child! I have
suffered from a narrow life; but that is the lot, you
see, of all my brethren who have a young and active
disposition. I have spoken of this to make you understand that one can bear everything, that one can
even find happiness and cheerfulness when trials
have passed, if one bears them courageously."

I understood him perfectly, but the curé was preach-
ing in the desert. I was too young not to be very
fixed in my ideas, and I naturally said to myself that
in the way of troubles nothing can compare with a
disappointment in love.

"If the living of Pavol is vacant some day, I should
be happy to go there, Reine, only I have no voice in
the matter."

"Yes, I know that; but my uncle is a great friend
of the bishop. He will arrange it."

The curé drove me back to C——. When he saw
me installed in my uncle's elegant landau, he cried:

"How happy I am to see you in your proper place,
Reine! This landau makes a better setting for you
than Jean's cart!"

"You will soon see me in a beautiful château," I
answered. "I am going to pray the saints that the

curé of Pavol may fly away to heaven; it is a very charitable wish, because he is old and ill. You will have a beautiful church and a pulpit, Monsieur le Curé,—a real high pulpit!"

The horses started, and I leaned over the door to see the last of my old curé, who waved me adieus without thinking of putting on his hat, for a blissful and joyous hope had entered his heart.

CHAPTER XVII.

THIS visit to the curé did me good for a time only.

The salutary effect of his counsels vanished rapidly. I fell back into my gloomy fancies; and my uncle, all the while inwardly cursing womankind, nieces, their obstinacy, and their caprices, spoke of taking us to Paris, Blanche and me, for a change of scene, when most happily events came with a rush.

A few days after this, Monsieur de Pavol received a letter from a friend, who asked permission to bring to the château one of his cousins,— a Monsieur de Kerveloch, an old *attaché* of the embassy.

My uncle answered promptly that he would be happy to receive Monsieur de Kerveloch, and invited him to breakfast without suspecting that he was hastening an event which, while it destroyed his pet scheme, would restore my hopes and happiness.

The next day but one, — I have good reason to always remember that famous day, — the next day but one, the weather was atrocious.

According to our custom, we were all in the salon. Blanche, thoughtful, seated near the fire, answered Monsieur de Conprat in monosyllables.

This headstrong lover, not being able to bear his exile, had reappeared at Pavol forty-eight hours before. My uncle read his paper; and as for me, I had taken refuge in a window-recess.

Now I worked with a nervous activity, for I was devoted to needle-work; now I watched the leaden sky, and the rain which fell without stopping. I heard the wind roar, — that November wind which wails in such melancholy fashion, — and I felt tired and sad without the least presentiment of happiness, although at that very moment happiness was coming to me behind a fine pair of fast-trotting horses.

From time to time I threw a stealthy glance of the eye at Paul. He was watching Blanche with a look which made me want to strangle him.

"What a stupid he looks like," I said to myself, "with his staring, sheepish eyes glued on her! Yes; but if I were in Blanche's place, and he looked at me in the same way, I should think him charming and more attractive than ever! Such is human stupidity and inconsistency."

And I drove my needle with such fury that it broke off short.

At that moment we heard a carriage approach the château. My uncle folded up his paper; Juno pricked up her ears, saying, "Here comes some one;" and a few seconds after my uncle's friend and his *attaché* of the embassy appeared.

I do not know why in my mind this title was inseparable from old age and baldness. Nevertheless, not only was Monsieur de Kerveloch neither old nor bald, but with the exception of Francis I. as shown in his portrait, I have never seen a man of such fine physique.

When he entered, I had an idea that he had matrimonial designs in his handsome head. He was thirty years old, and was so tall that beside him Paul seemed transformed into a pygmy; his expression was intelligent, haughty, and such that no one at first sight, or even at second sight, would have assigned him the aureole of a saint. Reserved, but courteous to a degree, he had polished manners, and an ease which captivated Blanche on the spot.

Monsieur de Kerveloch watched her with admiration; and when he rose to go away, and stood before her, I felt with a secret joy that a better-assorted couple could not be seen.

I think each one had the same idea, for Paul left us with a gloomy face. Juno played over Weber's

Last Thought, or something equally tiresome, ten
times in succession,—a proof with her of great absent-
mindedness; while my uncle watched each of us with
a thoughtful and satirical air.

Monsieur de Kerveloch came to breakfast the next
day at Pavol; three days after, he proposed for Blanche;
and two weeks later I wrote to the curé,—

My dear Curé, — Man is an inconstant, changeable, capri-
cious little animal, a weathercock which veers to all the whims
of imagination and circumstance. When I say man, I mean
to speak of humanity in general, because I am to-day the
little animal in question.

I am in despair no longer. I have no more desire to die,
my curé. I find that the sun has recovered its brilliancy; that
the future holds many pleasures for me; that the universe is
wise in existing, and that death is the most stupid invention
of the Creator.

Blanche is to marry, Monsieur le Curé! Blanche is to
marry the Comte de Kerveloch! *Dieu!* how well they suit
each other! And it was only by a straw, a hair's breadth, by
nothing at all, that she missed accepting Monsieur de Conprat,
—a man she did not love, and whom she found fault with for
eating too much. Eating too much,— it is absurd, such an
idea! as if it were not perfectly rational to eat heartily when
one has a good appetite. If you ask me how matters have
changed so suddenly at Pavol, I can hardly answer you. I am
entirely upset; and all that I can tell you is that one beautiful
day, one superb day,— no, it was raining in torrents, but that
is no matter,—one day, I say, Monsieur de Kerveloch came
here, brought by a friend of my uncle. When I saw him enter,

I fancied that he had some ulterior motive, fancied also that he would please Blanche, because he has all the qualities she dreams of in a husband. Monsieur de Kerveloch looked at her as a man who knows how to appreciate beauty; and some days after he solicited the honour of her hand, as my uncle and etiquette express it.

Juno shook off her usual nonchalance to declare with warmth that no suitor had ever pleased her as much, and that she had fully decided to refuse Monsieur de Conprat.

That is the story, my dear curé. It is plain, simple, clear; and since then my fancies soar as in the past. I throw the reins on the neck of my imagination and let it canter and canter until it can go no longer; and I dance in my room when I am all alone. Ah, my dear curé, I do not know why I love you to-day ten times more than usual. Your good face seems to me more smiling than ever, your affection more touching, more delightful, your beautiful white hair more charming.

This morning I looked at the leafless trees, which seemed to me fresh and green, at the gray sky, which seemed quite blue, and all at once I made friends with my imagination. I shall repent all my life of having treated it so villanously the other day. It is a fairy, my dear curé, — a fairy full of charm, of power, of poetry, which, touching the ugliest things with its magic wand, clothes them with its own beauty.

What a changeable little being it is! I cannot get over it. Why cherish hope and joy? Why make one's self wretched when things arrange themselves so well without one's interference? But why am I so light-hearted when nothing is yet decided as to my future, and when I remember that it is not possible to love twice in the course of one's life. What a chaos, my curé! The world is full of mysteries, and the soul is a fathomless abyss. I believe that some one, I do not know where, has already uttered this thought, perhaps even I read it no later than yesterday, but I was perfectly able to say as much.

Nevertheless, when my excitement subsides, my joyful hopes are seized with an irresistible panic; they escape, fly away, and disappear, and I often cannot call them back. Because, after all, he loves her, Monsieur le Curé; he loves her, — a wretched word used as I use it now.

You said to me that it was not unusual to be in love twice in a lifetime, my curé; but are you sure? Are you perfectly certain? Love attracts love, they say; if he knew my secret, would he, perhaps, love me? You, who are a man of sense, Monsieur le Curé, do you not find the proprieties idiotic? An avowal on my part would probably be enough to secure the happiness of my whole life; and here are these rules, invented by some one without judgment, which prevent my following my inclination to reveal my secret thoughts and tell my love to him I love. To speak the truth, something, I know not what, at the bottom of my heart, compels me as strongly to be silent and — did I not say to you that the soul was a fathomless abyss! My dear curé, I see a procession of gloomy fancies approaching. How ill-balanced man is!

There is no doubt that circumstances modify opinions. My uncle goes so far as to assert that fools only never change their minds; but is it the same with the heart as the mind?

Enlighten me, my old curé.

When a thing was decided on, Monsieur de Pavol never liked to dilly-dally in carrying it out. In accordance with this principle he decided that Blanche's marriage should take place January 15.

His misapprehension had been a rude shock; but he was the less disposed to oppose his daughter because he knew of my love, and because he was generous, upright, intelligent, and incapable of persisting in any pet project when the happiness of his niece was at stake.

As to Paul, he bore his ill-fortune bravely. Like the little creature who loved him so tenderly without his suspecting it, he had not the smallest particle of angry feeling. I certify that he never had a desire to poison his rival or gallantly cut his throat in some lonely and poetic nook in the woods.

When he knew that his hopes were ruined, he came to see us with the commandant. He held out his hand to Blanche, saying in a generous and natural tone, —

"Cousin, I wish only your happiness, and I hope we shall continue good friends."

But this way of acting the comedy hero did not prevent his being greatly disappointed. His visits to Pavol became very rare; and when I saw him, I thought him changed mentally and physically.

Then I wept anew in secret, feeling very angry at him. It would have been so logical to love me, so rational to see that our two characters were prodigiously alike, and that I loved him to distraction. Truly if men were always logical, the world would be no worse, and their dispositions would be much better.

CHAPTER XVIII.

THE 15th of January was beautiful and very cold. The fields, covered with hoar-frost, looked like fairyland. Juno, though very pale, was so beautiful in her white dress that I could not keep my eyes off her. She seemed to me like the cold and magnificent world without, which, robed in dazzling white, was in keeping with her beauty.

After the breakfast she went to her room to change her dress. She came down greatly agitated; we kissed her tearfully; and she was off for Italy.

"The happy moment, the happy moment!" I said to myself.

My many emotions had tired me out, and I wanted to be alone. So leaving my uncle to dispose of his guests as he best could, I caught up a fur cloak and set out for a spot in the park of which I was especially fond.

The park was crossed by a swift and narrow stream; at a certain part of its course it broadened out and formed a cascade which some skilfully arranged rocks made high and picturesque. A little way from the cascade a tree had fallen, its foot on one side of the stream, its top on the other. It had been forgotten as it lay; and when, the next spring, my uncle wanted to take it away, he saw that it was alive by the vigorous branches which were shooting out all along its trunk. He had another tree thrown beside it, intertwined their branches, planted convolvulus, which was trained over the two, and in course of time branches and convolvulus became so thick that my uncle had an original rustic bridge which could be crossed without the least danger of any one's getting entangled in the branches and falling into the water.

It was this lonely spot, at some distance from the château, which I had chosen as the scene of my meditations. I stopped near the frost-covered bridge to reflect on the future and admire the enormous icicles hanging at the cascade which the cold had frozen as the water fell.

I do not know how long I was meditating thus without noticing the cold which stung my face, when I saw approaching the "object of my affection," as Madame Cottin would say.

The "object" appeared to be melancholy and in a very bad humour; with a cane which in a moment of abstraction he had stolen from my uncle, he dealt energetic blows at the trees which came in his way, and the white dust which covered them was scattered over him.

I half turned about; but it is well known that women have eyes in the backs of their heads, and I did not miss one of his movements.

When he came near he crossed his arms, looked at the motionless cascade, the bridge, the trees, but did not open his mouth. Busy with a little fir twig which I was breaking off, I held my breath, watching him sideways without his knowing it.

"Cousin!"

"Cousin!"

I waited some seconds for him to conclude his remarks; but finding that he stopped there, I condescended to turn half about toward the speaker, to encourage him.

He scowled and burst out,—

"I should like to blow my brains out!"

"Very well," I said dryly; "I will go to your funeral."

This reply surprised him so much that he dropped his arms and stared at me.

"You would not keep me from committing suicide, Cousin?"

"Certainly not," I answered tranquilly. "Why should I mix myself in what does not concern me? I love liberty; and if you desire to quit this vale of tears,— *eh, mon Dieu!* — I would not raise a finger to stop you. Let every one in this world do as he pleases."

With that I set about considering my fir twig again, while "my object," disconcerted by the liberal way in which I had regarded his lugubrious plan, had a somewhat disconcerted air.

"I thought you had a little regard for me, Mademoiselle ma Cousine. The first time you saw me you thought me agreeable."

"Alas, Monsieur mon Cousin! what signifies the liking of a little country girl who is reduced to the society of a curé, a scolding aunt, and a cross-grained cook?"

"Which means that you were nice to me simply because I was not a curé, and my face was not entirely withered like that of Madame de Lavalle?"

"You have said it, fair cousin."

He looked at me with fury, twisting his mustache viciously, and seizing his hat, threw it angrily on the bridge. Oh, how well I understood the action of his mind! He was delighted,—delighted to find a pretext to growl, and to blame me for his deception, just as I had vented my bitterness on my terracotta men and the unfortunate Baron Le Maltour.

"Your aunt was horrible, Mademoiselle!" he said brusquely.

"My beautiful eyes made up for it, Monsieur," I answered in the same tone.

"And what a charming table and lovely service! Everything was criss-cross!"

"Yes; but what a turkey! How was it you did not die of indigestion? I really thought you had, until I saw you here — *mon Dieu!* — in perfect health." ·

"I know that it is impossible to have the last word with you, Mademoiselle; I am not, for all that, altogether unbearable, Cousin. What have I done to you?"

"Nothing at all! I have proved that by promising to accompany your body to its last resting-place."

"My body!" he cried with a painful shiver. "I am not yet dead, Mademoiselle. Understand that I do not intend to kill myself, and that I am about to set out for Russia."

"Bon voyage, Monsieur mon Cousin!"

He went away; and thinking that he was gone for a very long time, I crossed my hands dejectedly and great tears were coming to my eyes, when I saw him running back.

"Come, Reine, let us not sulk, either of us. Why were you an — Why, are you crying?"

"I was thinking of Juno," I said, succeeding in speaking in a natural tone.

"That is true, little cousin; you will be entirely alone. Let us shake hands, shall we?"

"Willingly, Paul."

Alas! he did not kiss my hand; he only pressed it in melancholy fashion, because he was thinking of a fairer hand which he had dreamed of possessing.

And he went away for good and all.

Notwithstanding the cold, which I took no thought of, I sat down near the bridge in tears, and leaning over the stream, watched them fall on the ice.

"To speak of blowing out his brains!" I said, "he must love her prodigiously. I know that he will not; but he is probably as infatuated with her as I with him, and I am sure that I could never forget him. How silly it is! how silly it is! — to fall in love with a woman who is so ill-suited to him, while close at hand there is a little —"

"What are you doing here, Reine?" said my uncle, who had drawn near without my having heard his step.

I rose quickly, ashamed of not being able to hide my emotion.

"What! we are crying!"

"How stupid men are, Uncle!"

"A profound truth, my niece! Is that why you are crying?"

"Paul wants to blow his brains out," I said, weeping.

"Do you believe him capable of proceeding to such extremities?"

"No," I answered, smiling in spite of my tears. "Violence is certainly contrary to his nature; but his wish proves that —"

"Yes, I know, my niece. His wish shows that he loves my daughter; but, believe me, he will forget her very quickly, and when he returns here we will take such steps that his heart shall not go astray again."

"You think, then, Uncle, that a man can love twice in his life without being a phenomenon?"

Monsieur de Pavol patted my cheek and looked at me with a commiseration addressed as much to my inexperience as to my trouble.

"Poor little niece! The men who love only once in a life are as little known as the peak of Aiguille-Verte."

"Then, Uncle, man is a wretched creature," I said with conviction.

But I was as enchanted as indignant, and I asked nothing better than to profit by the inherent villany of human nature.

"But Juno is so beautiful!"

"Look at this bridge which you are so fond of,

Reine. Before the branches and the plants which cover it are green again, Paul will have forgotten; before the leaves have had time to turn yellow and fall again, he will have returned to Pavol, and — "

He smiled significantly, and took himself off without finishing his sentence; while I, quite startled, watched him disappear, thinking that uncles who predict the future with so much self-possession are truly singular beings.

"It is all very well," I said, retaking with slow steps the path to the house; "but if his heart changes, he can be infatuated with some woman on his travels. And, in fact, they say that Russian women are very beautiful — He must be sent among the Eskimos."

I began to run with all my might, and reached the door of the château just as the commandant was getting into his carriage.

I took his arm and led him one side.

"Commandant, Paul is going to Russia?"

"Yes; his journey is decided on."

"I thought — if you liked that — in short, it would be better — "

Decidedly it was much more difficult to speak out than I had supposed. My pride stood in the way and urged me to be silent.

"Well, dear child, speak quickly; I am freezing here!"

"The die is cast!" I cried aloud, stamping my foot.

My pride and I crossed the Rubicon, and I said, dropping my eyes,—

"My dear commandant, I beg you, advise Paul to go among the Eskimos."

"Why among the Eskimos?"

"Because the women of that country are hideous, and the Russians are very beautiful."

The good commandant raised my face, all red with confusion, and answered simply,—

"So be it; I shall advise him to go among the Eskimos."

"How I love you!" I said, tears in my eyes as I pressed his hand. "But tell him not to stay long in the huts of those good people and get ill; it seems that there is a most atrocious smell —"

Seeing my uncle approach, I fled, saying,—

"Commandant, a man of honour has but to give his word. Be sure and keep yours."

I went up to my room with the very disagreeable assurance that I had followed fully the example of the government, and that I had trodden under foot all considerations of dignity.

But, bah! if one does not help one's self a little in this world, how can one be able to take advantage of an opportunity? This reflection suppressed my compunctions. I sat down at my secretary and wrote:

"All is over, Monsieur le Curé! They are married; they have gone, happy and blissful; and I would have given ten years of my existence to be in Juno's place, with him whom you well know.   When shall I be there ?

" Do you know what my uncle said?   He asserts that men who love only once in their life are as little known as the peak of Aiguille-Verte.   My curé, my dear curé, I beg you, pray to-morrow that Monsieur de Conprat be not the peak of Aiguille-Verte.

" Au revoir, Monsieur le Curé ; I hope you will come soon to the living of Pavol."

16

CHAPTER XIX.

THE only event of the end of the winter was, in fact, the installation of the curé in the parish of Pavol, and I will not dwell on the happiness we had in finding ourselves without fear of a near separation.

With what delight did I see him enter the pulpit, and preach, with a joyous air, on the iniquities of man. Then he came to the château, as of old to Buisson, his cassock tucked up, his hat under his arm, his hair blowing in the wind.

We resumed our talks, our arguments, our disputes. The time seemed to me very long; and Juno's letters, which breathed the most complete happiness, were not of a kind to console and make me patient. So I went continually to find the curé, to confide to him my cares, my anxieties, my hopes, and my impatience at the delay which I had to endure.

I knew that "my object" had not in the least approved the idea of going among the Eskimos. He was wandering tranquilly about St. Petersburg, and the beautiful Russian ladies frightened me terribly.

"Are you sure that he will not fall in love with a Russian, Monsieur le Curé?"

"We will hope so, little Reine."

"We will hope so! Answer more categorically, my curé! What are you thinking of? Come, it is not possible that he should fall in love with a foreigner; tell me that it is not, and that he will love me some day!"

"I hope so sincerely, my poor little child; but you would do better to think otherwise and act accordingly."

"You will worry me to death with your resignation, my dear curé."

"Ah, how little wisdom you have, Reine!"

"Wisdom, in my opinion, consists in wishing for happiness. Tell me that he will love me, my curé, I beg you."

"I ask nothing better, my dear child," answered the curé, who, notwithstanding his dread of physical suffering, would have been perfectly capable of following the example of Mucius Scævola and burning his right hand, if my happiness had depended on such a sacrifice.

None the less, notwithstanding the joy of having my

curé, notwithstanding the kindness of my uncle and all those about me, I became very depressed.

I loved to wander alone through the paths of the wood. I loved to stay by the hour near the cascade, thinking of our last meeting, thinking what I should do if I saw him appear, bright and charming, with his eyes full of that look which had pleased me so much at Buisson, and which I had never since seen in them for me.

This love of solitude increased day by day, and my melancholy increased in proportion. At last I lost, little by little, my talkativeness; and if Monsieur de Pavol had not now for a long time believed in the sincerity of my love, this fact alone would have proved its depth.

Six months passed in this way.

One day, the anniversary of my arrival at Pavol, I was seated in the garden of the *presbytère.* A shower, two hours before, had refreshed the air and bathed the curé's flowers. He was amusing himself in looking for snails; while I, under the influence of pleasant thoughts, leaned my head against the wall near which my bench was placed, and let joyful hopes take possession of me. The drops of water, which bent down the leaves under their weight, alone disturbed my meditations as they fell, and the odour of the wet earth recalled the happiest hours of my life.

From time to time the curé said to me, —

"It is astonishing, — all these snails! Would you

believe, Reine, that I have already found more than five hundred?"

I lifted my head carelessly, and smilingly watched the good curé, who continued his researches with ardour. Then I betook myself again to my reveries, and ended by falling half asleep.

I was awakened by the scraping of the gate in the garden-hedge and the sound of a cheerful voice which gave me the most violent start I ever had.

"Good-day, my dear curé; how do you do? How pleased I am to see you! And Reine, where is she?"

Reine was still seated in the same place, finding it impossible to speak or move.

"Ah, there she is!" cried Paul, approaching with long strides. "Dear little cousin, how happy I am, — *mon Dieu*, how happy I am to see you!"

He took my hand and kissed it.

I declare that what followed was entirely independent of my will, and that it is not necessary to make unkind inferences with respect to me.

I declare that I fought against temptation with all my might. But when I felt his lips on my hand; when I realized that the act was not inspired by ordinary gallantry, but by a deeper feeling; when I saw him bend over me and look at me with an anxious, singular, affectionate expression, a hundred times more enchanting than what I had dreamed of, — it was too much for my strength; and fate, in which I have been a believer from that moment, picked me up and threw me into his arms.

I had hardly time to feel the embrace that responded to my outburst. I took refuge, red and confused, on the bench, hiding my face in my hands, not without having caught a glimpse of the face of the curé, whose stupefied, frightened, delighted look came back to me afterward.

"Dear Reine," Paul murmured in my ear, "if I had known your secret sooner, I should not have stayed so long away from you."

I did not answer, for I was weeping.

He took one of my hands by force and held it in his; while, overcome by an attack of timidity such as I had never had, I turned my head aside, trying to withdraw it.

"Let me have it, this pretty little hand; it belongs to me now. Turn your head this way, Reine."

I looked straight into those beautiful honest eyes which smiled at me, and cried,—

"Heaven be praised! my uncle was right; you are not the peak of Aiguille-Verte!"

"The peak of Aiguille-Verte!" he exclaimed, astonished.

"Yes; my uncle asserted — but no matter! Who told you what you did not know when you went away?"

"My father, Monsieur de Pavol, and many things which recurred to me during the last two months."

" It is true, then, that love attracts love?" I said innocently.

" Nothing is more true, dear little *fiancée!*"

Oh, the sweet name ! Yes, we were engaged; and we were silent, while the curé wept for joy, the sparrows on the roof of the *presbytère* chattered deafeningly, and the snails, escaping from the prison where the curé had placed them, ran in every direction.

Most certainly the sparrow is not a fascinating bird; its plumage is dull and ugly, its note lacks sweetness, and some persons declare that it is a thief and immoral, which I refuse to believe. I do not know further that snails have passed for very poetic animals; it is none the less true that from the moment of which I am speaking, I have adored sparrows and snails.

I was in an ecstasy; I thought myself in a dream. I did not take my eyes off him, as I listened to the voice I loved so well and felt my hand grasped in his. All the same, in spite of myself, the recollection of her whom he had loved haunted my mind and troubled my joy a little, though I did not dare to speak of it.

" My uncle knows that you are here, Paul? "

" Yes, I come from Pavol; and I wished to come to you absolutely alone. This wet garden, does it recall anything to you, Reine? "

I did not answer his question directly. I said to him only,—

"But you — you retained a bad impression of Buisson?"

"I, indeed! I never passed so pleasant an evening."

"Oh," I went on, watching him slyly, "my aunt, who was horrible?"

"No, no, not so horrible. A little common, perhaps; but you seemed only the more charming for it."

"And the cover so badly laid, everything criss-cross!"

"I never dined so well. That dilapidated interior made you appear like a flower which seems prettier and more delicate because the plot in which it sprung is ugly and unkempt."

"You have become a poet on your travels," I said, smiling.

"No, not in the least, little Reine."

He put my arm in his and led me aside.

"No, not a poet, but your lover. Cousin, hear me; I love you sincerely and with all my heart."

I enjoyed the sweet words and the look which accompanied them, saying to myself inwardly that it was most fortunate that men were inconstant.

But the change appeared to me unheard of, and I could not help saying,—

"Is it certain that you do not love her any more at all, at all?"

"Would I speak as I have if it were not so?" he answered seriously. "Have you not confidence in my loyalty?"

" Oh, yes ! " I exclaimed, crossing my hands on his arm in an outburst of affection.

It was perfectly true, for after his answer the image of Blanche never rose to trouble me. I loved him without a thought of the past, of jealousy or distrust ; and he deserved this perfect confidence.

" Ah, here come my father and Monsieur de Pavol."

" Well, my niece, what do you think of my prediction ? "

" You are not very discreet, Uncle," I said, blushing.

" It was the commandant who revealed the secret, Reine ; he has known it for a long time."

" Oh, no, only for eight months."

" From the first day when I saw you, dear little daughter."

" Is it possible ? "

" And Paul did not go at all among the Eskimos," added my uncle, laughing.

How delightful it is to live among kind hearts ! I felt this pleasure keenly as I saw with what satisfaction they all shared my joy, with what delicacy, what kindliness, they jested about that famous secret which, without suspecting it, I had proclaimed to all the winds.

Then began that enchanting time, — the time when one is engaged, that delicious period which has nothing like it in life. Nothing can take the place of those hours of innocent love, of trust, of perfect illusions, and of youthful fancies. Ah, how I pity those who have never

loved in this way! How I pity those whose folly draws
them far from the common path and pure affection!
And as to that, never, never, no matter what may be
the eloquence of those who wish to convince me, will I
believe that true love can exist without having respect
as its basis.

We passed our days most delightfully at the *presbytère*, under the chaperonage of the curé. We watched
him bustling about his garden, fastening his plants to
their stakes, pulling up weeds, and stopping in his work
to throw an inquiring glance in our direction, in order
to let us know that he was a serious mentor.

We smiled at each other because we knew the sever-
ity of our debonair guardian.

I would go and fall in ecstasies with him over some
flower, shrub, or fruit, and would say,—

"My curé, do you remember the time when you
tried to persuade me that love was not the most charming thing in the world?"

"Ah, my little child, I believe that Bossuet himself
could not have convinced you."

"Come, was I not right?"

"I begin to believe so," he would answer with his
good and charming smile.

The day of my marriage dawned radiant for me.
Never had the vault of heaven seemed more splendid.
Since then I have been told that it was cloudy; but I
believe none of it.

A throng of friends filled the church. There were whispers,—

"What a lovely bride! How happy and tranquil she seems!"

It is true that I was surprisingly calm.

But why should I have disquieted myself? My most cherished dream had come true; a future of happiness opened before me; and not the lightest anxiety came to trouble me.

I saw indistinctly some dowagers smiling as I passed; and I was seized with a great compassion, as I reflected that they were too old to be married.

The organ resounded so joyously that at the time I overcame a little of my prejudice against music. The altar was adorned with flowers and dazzling with lights, and all the details of decoration under the artistic taste of Juno charmed the eye.

My husband put the wedding ring on my finger with an uncertain hand, biting his beautiful mustache to hide his trembling lips. He was much more affected than I, and his look said what I should have loved to have said over and over without end.

And truly one might have searched the world over, and all the other planets of the universe, to find a face as radiant as that of my curé.

THE END.